SPURT

CHRIS MILES

Simon & Schuster Books for Young Readers

New York   London   Toronto   Sydney   New Delhi

SIMON & SCHUSTER BOOKS FOR YOUNG READERS
An imprint of Simon & Schuster Children's Publishing Division
1230 Avenue of the Americas, New York, New York 10020
This book is a work of fiction. Any references to historical events,
real people, or real places are used fictitiously. Other names, characters, places,
and events are products of the author's imagination, and any resemblance to
actual events or places or persons, living or dead, is entirely coincidental.
Text copyright © 2014 by Chris Miles
Originally published in Australia in 2014 by Hardie Grant Egmont
Published by arrangement with Hardie Grant Egmont, Australia
First U.S. edition February 2017
Reverse-side jacket images copyright © 2017 by Thinkstock
All rights reserved, including the right of reproduction in whole or in part in
any form.
SIMON & SCHUSTER BOOKS FOR YOUNG READERS is a trademark of
Simon & Schuster, Inc.
For information about special discounts for bulk purchases, please contact Simon &
Schuster Special Sales at 1-866-506-1949 or business@simonandschuster.com.
The Simon & Schuster Speakers Bureau can bring authors to your live event. For
more information or to book an event, contact the Simon & Schuster Speakers
Bureau at 1-866-248-3049 or visit our website at www.simonspeakers.com.
Book design and outside jacket illustration by Lucy Ruth Cummins
The text for this book was set in Adobe Garamond Pro.
Manufactured in the United States of America | 0117 FFG
10 9 8 7 6 5 4 3 2 1
Library of Congress Cataloging-in-Publication Data
Names: Miles, Chris, author.
Title: Spurt / Chris Miles.
Description: First edition. | New York : Simon & Schuster Books for Young
Readers, [2017] | Summary: Eighth-grader Jack, a former reality television
star and distressed at not reaching puberty, decides to "fake it until he makes it."
Identifiers: LCCN 2016003375 |
ISBN 9781481479721 (hardcover) | ISBN 9781481479745 (eBook)
Subjects: | CYAC: Puberty—Fiction. | Friendship—Fiction. | Reality television
programs—Fiction. | Junior high schools—Fiction. | Schools—Fiction. |
Humorous stories.
Classification: LCC PZ7.1.M5564 Sp 2017 | DDC [Fic]—dc23
LC record available at https://lccn.loc.gov/2016003375

For Nikki, who changed everything

Part One

Pubelessly Blue

Chapter One

Jack Sprigley stared down his pajama bottoms on the first morning of spring semester and realized that his worst fears had come true.

Nothing had changed.

No last-minute dash to the finish line. No final charge across the battlefield to victory. No champagne-cork-popping moment that meant he'd joined the rest of eighth grade in all its hairy, pimply glory.

He snapped the pajama elastic back.

Time had run out. Another school year was nearly over.

And he was still stranded on Pubeless Island.

Jack sat at the kitchen table with a bigger-than-usual bowl of cornflakes. His mom, Adele, glanced up at him from her cup of tea.

"First day back," she said.

"Yep," said Jack.

His mom took a sip of her tea. "Must be looking forward to seeing everyone again?"

Jack shrugged. "Sure."

Hallie breezed past and grabbed her breakfast smoothie from the fridge.

"It's just that you did seem to spend most of the break shut away in your room," said Jack's mom, not quite making eye contact. "On your own," she added.

"Gross," said Hallie from the other side of the fridge door.

"I was busy," said Jack.

"Gross," said Hallie.

Jack could guess what his sister was thinking. A fourteen-year-old boy, alone in his room for days—there were natural conclusions to be drawn.

But that was the problem. Guessing was all he *could* do. Sure, everything Ms. Porter talked about in Health Ed made total sense.

In theory.

"Anyway," said Jack. "It's not like we had zero contact, we just . . . hung out online."

"Right," said his mom, definitely not convinced. "So you hung out with Vivi, Reese, and Darylyn online."

"Uh-huh," Jack said through a mouthful of cereal.

Jack's gran, Marlene, shuffled into the kitchen and switched the kettle on. "Don't forget to take my prescription to the drugstore today, Jack."

"I never have forgotten, Gran," said Jack, relieved at the change of subject.

He finished his bigger-than-usual bowl of cornflakes in silence.

So far, Jack had come up with three possible reasons for his freakish lack of progress in the man-parts department:

1) His body was building up to a massive growth spurt. At some point soon he'd turn into an Incredible Hulk of puberty and sprout a pair of really enormous testicles.

2) It was a punishment from the gods for becoming semifamous in sixth grade.

3) There'd been a mix-up at the hospital and he was actually a girl.

Jack had already ruled out 2. If gods existed, they probably had better things to do than watch reality TV. If it was 3, and he was a girl, the situation was still pretty messed up because he didn't have any boobs or anything either.

Even if it was 1, and he ended up with gamma-charged

superjunk, Jack had a feeling it might be too late. He was pretty sure his friends had already dumped him.

The signs were obvious. Vivi hadn't called or e-mailed or even messaged since the end of last semester. Two whole weeks of silence. To which Jack had responded with . . . well, to be fair, silence.

No word from Reese, either. Not a single link to a fuzzy YouTube clip of whichever obscure sixties garage rock band or scuzzy rockabilly weirdos were rotating highly on his playlist that week.

Ditto Darylyn. Not even a reply to Jack's text asking her to switch his laptop back to how it had been before she'd "improved" it.

Nothing.

His mom was right. Jack hadn't seen his friends for two weeks.

It wasn't just the freeze-out over the break, though. Sometime around the end of seventh grade, Jack had started noticing the changes. Darylyn's pimples. The hair above Reese's lip and under his arms. Vivi becoming, to the extent that Jack had looked, more "boobs-having."

There'd been other things too. A week before the end of first semester, he'd caught Reese and Darylyn whispering to each other when they were all hanging out together at the Ninth Street Mall after school. He hadn't thought much of it at the time. Now he realized: That must have been the moment they'd started to question if they could really afford to be seen in public with someone who looked more "kid brother" than "homie." At some point the seeds of doubt must have been planted in Vivi's mind too.

Now everything seemed to have come to a head, like the pus in one of the pimples that everyone but him seemed to have on their faces now. Vivi, Reese, and Darylyn had obviously gotten together as soon as first semester had ended and decided to ditch Jack. Because that was what happened when you didn't measure up.

You got left behind.

Jack jammed his laptop into his backpack and stuffed his shorts, Nike Zooms, and water bottle in too.

He'd really hoped his growth spurt might hit by the time school went back. Everything Jack had read on forums and message boards over the break said his time would come. Eventually his hormones would kick into action and he'd transform from pubeless weirdo freak-boy to socially acceptable, testosterone-packing man-beast.

But Jack didn't have time for eventually. He'd already passed up his chance to become Mr. Popular after being on TV—and now it looked like he'd been ditched by the few friends he *did* have. Complete social rejection was a mere pube's-breadth away.

He had to buy himself some time.

That was when Jack thought of *Bigwigs*. Sure, it had been two whole years since he'd been in front of the cameras. Sure, it was just a dumb game show. But it got him thinking. Bigwigs had been about pretending you were something you weren't. Teams of kids were sent out into workplaces week after week, doing jobs that adults would normally do. And the better the contestants played at being adults, the further they went on the show.

Pretending. Was the answer as simple as that?

Jack slung his backpack over one shoulder and headed out the back door and down the side walkway to the street, spurred by his stroke of genius.

If he wanted to stay tight with Vivi and the others, all he had to do was commit a relatively simple act of deception. All he had to do was convince his friends he *had* hit his growth spurt.

All he had to do, basically, was *fake puberty*.

uys!"

Vivi, Reese, and Darylyn were just about to dis-appear through the school gate. As Jack got nearer, he noticed Vivi tighten her grip on the strap of her schoolbag, as if it were a ripcord she could pull to parachute herself out of the situation.

"Hey, Jack," she said. "We were going to wait for you. . . ."

"No need," said Jack. "I caught up. *T-o-o-tally* caught up."

Darylyn swept her bangs out of her eyes.

"I got your text about the laptop." Darylyn always spoke super fast, as though the act of speech were like ripping off a Band-Aid. She glanced sideways at Reese, who kept his eyes stubbornly fixed on his black-and-white-checked Vans. "I forgot to reply."

Jack shrugged. "That's cool. "'Cos, yeah. It turns out I was too busy to use the computer much anyway."

"Busy?" said Vivi.

"Yeah," said Jack, staring manfully into the distance and nodding. He turned back to the others. "Sorry if I kind of . . . dropped off the radar."

Vivi frowned. "What kind of busy?"

"Just . . . you know," Jack said significantly. "Going through a bit of *man* stuff."

"What does that mean?" asked Vivi.

Jack froze. What *did* he mean? "You know. Just your typical guy stuff. Reese, you know what it's like."

If Darylyn Deramo was a fast talker, Reese Rasmus was the opposite. He was inclined to think very deeply about things. In fact, sometimes he thought so deeply about things that listening to him speak was a bit like listening to someone trying to invent the whole concept of language from scratch.

"Um . . . ," he said.

Jack nodded understandingly in a "we're both in this testosterone thing together" kind of way. "Look, it's cool if you don't want to go into detail. You know, with the ladies present."

"It's not that, dude," said Reese, frowning. "I seriously don't know what you're talking about."

Jack sighed. "Come on, guys. It's obvious what I've been doing. We're all perfectly normal teenagers going through all the normal changes that normal teenagers go through at this age. You know?"

Vivi frowned. "Not reall—"

"Masturbating," said Jack, desperately.

Vivi's mouth dropped open. Darylyn took an involuntary step backward. Reese's brow crinkled. "Dude . . . ," he said.

Jack faltered. It was clear he'd brought out the big guns too soon. But he was committed now. There was nothing to do but keep firing away. "Y-yeah. Just . . . a whole ton of masturbating, really."

There was a difficult pause. Jack thought he heard Reese say "Dude" again under his breath.

Jack shrugged and tried to act casual. "That's pretty normal, though. I mean, we're all growing up so goddamn *fast*, right? Half the time we can't even control what our bodies are *doing*. It's like . . . UFOs could land and I'd be concentrating so hard on masturbating myself silly I wouldn't even notice. I'd look up and be all, 'Wow, first contact with aliens. Yeah, I get that it's important and everything, but this jerking off's not going to do itself!'"

Jack tried to ignore the looks he got from the group of seniors who'd overheard him as they walked through the gate. "So . . . yeah. I guess I've been pretty busy with all that. H-how was *your* break?"

The electronic chime of the homeroom bell rang out across the grounds of Upland Junior-Senior High.

Saved by the bell, thought Jack.

If the bell had rung at some point before he'd said the word "masturbating."

Reese steered Jack aside as they followed Vivi and Darylyn down the palm-lined main driveway toward the school hall. "Dude. *The entire break?*"

Jack chose to view the question as a positive sign. So far nobody had questioned his biological capacity for two weeks of whacking off. He had to be careful from now on, though. He didn't want to blow it all by making it obvious he had no idea what he was talking about.

"Oh yeah," said Jack. "Twenty times a day." *Seems plausible,* he thought.

Reese frowned. "So . . . you weren't hanging out with Vivi, then?"

"Well, no," said Jack. "Be a bit weird, wouldn't it? With all that masturbating going on. I mean, I'm no expert on girls—"

"Nah, me either," Reese said quickly. Then he seemed to catch himself, slowing his voice back down to regular Reese speed. "I mean, me either . . . dude."

"Wait," said Jack. "So you didn't see Vivi over the break either?"

Reese didn't seem to know where to look. "Um . . . maybe? When didn't *you* see her?"

"The whole time," said Jack, surprised that Reese even had to ask. "The primary reason being the nonstop masturbating."

"Dude, can you stop saying that?"

Jack took a moment to review the evidence. Did this mean there *wasn't* a conspiracy to ditch him? "So, wait . . . did you see Vivi or not?"

Reese hesitated. "S-sure. I guess we probably saw her . . . around?"

"We? Meaning you and Darylyn?"

Reese stopped. "Huh?"

"You said 'we.'" Jack noticed Reese looking fidgety. "And . . . now you're acting weird about it."

Reese seemed to be wrestling with something inside. He ran his hand through his fauxhawk and screwed up his face. "Listen, Jack, there's something I should—"

"There he is!" someone squealed.

Jack and Reese looked up to see three seventh graders in

Windbreakers and pleated skirts racing toward them across the asphalt of the school parking lot. They nudged Reese aside and huddled around Jack, sucking noisily on the plastic straws of their dome-lidded smoothie cups.

One of the girls pawed at Jack's sleeve with her free hand. "We've been voting for you!" she squeaked.

Voting for me? thought Jack. "What are you talking about?"

"A poll, on the *Bigwigs* forum," said the second girl, so excited she could barely stand still. The other two blew into their straws, making the sickly green smoothies bubble like the contents of a cauldron. "We stayed up clicking 'Jack, Jack, Jack' until it was time to go to bed!"

The third girl looked up from her smoothie and fixed Jack with a beady stare. "Nine thirty-five p.m. on school nights," she said in a deadly serious monotone.

"But . . . I'm not *on Bigwigs* anymore," said Jack.

The first girl rolled her eyes. "It's to see which finalists they should bring back, dummy!"

"Bring back—?"

The girls looked at one another, eyes wide, and shouted, "Bring back Jack! Bring back Jack!" in ear-piercing disharmony. Then they were gone, in a whirl of gingham and nylon.

Vivi waited with Darylyn while Jack and Reese caught

up with them again. "Fans of yours?" she asked Jack.

Jack shrugged. "Who knows?"

"They were clearly talking about *Bigwigs*," said Darylyn.

Jack feigned innocence. "Were they?"

Darylyn blinked. "It's impossible that you failed to hear that."

"I don't get it," said Vivi. "Why do you always freak out as soon as anyone brings up *Bigwigs*?"

Jack put on a look of false innocence. "I don't!"

"You do. Like last year, when they started showing the ads for the new season."

The show had only been on for two years, but they'd already changed the format and gone all meta. As well as kids going into real-life workplaces to do adult jobs, there'd been a mini-arc where the contestants had to produce an episode of *Bigwigs* itself. It had basically been the reality-TV equivalent of the movie *Inception*. Jack could only imagine what new schemes they were planning for the upcoming season.

"I didn't freak out," he said.

"You did," said Vivi.

Jack shrugged. "I don't know. I guess I just feel weird about it because it's a stupid kids' show. I've moved on. I've matured." He cast a meaningful glance downward. *"Big-time."*

Darylyn retreated behind her bangs and stared at the ground. Reese stuck his hands in his back pockets, cleared his throat, and looked away into the distance. Vivi just looked kind of puzzled and disappointed somehow.

"Anyway," said Vivi, after a short pause, "let's not go there again."

Jack was only half tuned in as everyone else started talking about what they were going to get for lunch later on. Mostly he was thinking about what the seventh-grade girls had said.

Bring back Jack?

What was *that* about?

Chapter Three

Jack and Vivi sat down next to each other in homeroom.

Way back at the beginning of eighth grade, Vivi would spend Monday mornings telling Jack all about some old subtitled movie she'd watched over the weekend. But it had been months since she'd asked Jack if he'd decided who his favorite classic on-screen cinema couple were. (Apparently King Kong and "the lady from *King Kong*" didn't count.)

Obviously she didn't think he was mature enough to discuss such topics anymore. Obviously he had to prove her wrong.

He leaned over to her. "You never said how your break was."

"It was . . . good," said Vivi. "Just, you know, thinking a few things over."

"Cool," said Jack. "I just wanted to check you hadn't tried to call or anything. Because obviously I was pretty busy with all this goddamn *puberty* stuff."

Vivi seemed distracted. She took a deep breath, tucked her hair behind her ears, and leaned closer to whisper to him. "Jack, I need to ask you something."

"O-okay," said Jack cautiously.

"I need to ask you if we're *friends*. I mean, really . . . *friends*."

It was the same question Jack had been asking himself since about halfway through the break. "I don't know. Are we?"

"Well, do you think that's what we *should* be?"

Jack nodded. It seemed like a no-brainer. "Oh yeah. Totally."

Vivi nodded too. "So, everything else . . . that's all just going to stay the way it is?"

Hopefully not everything *else,* thought Jack, pondering the depressingly stark tundra that greeted him on his visual safari down into his pajama bottoms every morning.

"I guess," he said.

Vivi stared at him for an uncomfortably long moment, nodded again, then returned to her side of the table.

Jack was still trying to figure out what had just happened

when Mr. Jacobs signaled for attention. On the board he'd written SECOND SEMESTER: STEPPING UP.

"Okay, 8C! A couple of pieces of business before you start this new term in your usual blaze of academic fervor. This semester, you begin your transition into ninth grade, which means you'll soon be choosing your subjects for next year. We'll be talking more about the Stepping Up program in the next couple of weeks. But the main thing to remember is this: It's time to start thinking about your futures."

The future? thought Jack. He wasn't ready for the future. Especially if it was going to involve conversations like the one he'd just had with Vivi.

On the surface, it seemed like Vivi had settled Jack's big fear. After all, she'd pretty much confirmed they were still friends. That everything was normal. That he wasn't in danger of becoming the saddest of social outcasts at Upland Junior High. But somehow it just didn't feel that way. Instead, it felt like the distance between them was getting wider.

"Speaking of stepping up," said Mr. Jacobs, "for those of you interested in applying for the Mayor for a Week program, the Community Engagement Committee is holding an information session tomorrow morning in the student center. There'll be someone from the mayor's office explaining the selection process, and one of our own ex-participants will be there to give you a taste of what the winner can expect."

"Mayor for a Week?" said Jack. "Sounds like a Vivi Dink-Dawson jam, most definitely."

Vivi looked thoughtfully out the window for a moment, then turned to Jack. "You think?"

"Are you serious? You've risen from hall monitor to international-student buddy to junior high captain. Your thirst for power is clearly unquenchable. Plus, how funny would it be to see you in those mayoral robes?"

Vivi smiled. "I do love me some civic regalia."

Jack smiled back. But he was still thinking about the confusing conversation they'd had at the beginning of homeroom. If they were still friends, why *had* she ignored him? Had something happened that she didn't want to tell him about? Maybe he just needed to man up and ask her directly.

"Listen, Vivi," said Jack in a low voice, "I was just thinking. Before, when you were asking if we're friends: I think I get it now."

"You do?"

Jack nodded. "Friends should feel like they can tell each other stuff, right?"

Vivi looked uncomfortable. "I guess?"

"Well, I'm guessing maybe there's something important you wanted to tell *me*. And I think—because I'm totally in the same place right now—I think I know what it is." Jack put on his most sincere face and leaned closer, hoping maybe to peer into Vivi's thoughts and divine the perfect thing to say. "Are you having *women's troubles?*"

Vivi pulled away. "Am I having *what?*"

Jack blinked. "Well, we're all in the middle of big changes in our lives, right? You, me, Reese, Darylyn . . . me . . . We're all growing up. Our minds, our bodies. Definitely mine are."

"*Women's* troubles, though? Are you from the . . . was there even a decade when people *said* that?"

"I just meant: I get it. It's a difficult period. I mean, n-not period. I mean, yes, *periods*, let's not deny the reality here, but—wait, where are you going?"

Vivi had collected her books and was leaving the table. Apparently the bell had rung. Everyone was on their way out the door.

Jack hadn't even noticed.

Jack barely said a word to Vivi during their first class—and not just because Ms. Liaw ran her Sociology class with a complete intolerance for socializing. So far, leaving aside one or two unfortunate word choices, he felt like his plan to convince everyone he'd hit puberty had gone pretty well. But after the weirdness with Vivi at the end of homeroom, he realized how easy it would be to undo all his good work. All he had to do was say the wrong thing—again—and he'd be sticking his neck under the friendship guillotine.

And that wasn't all he had to worry about. Jack couldn't stop thinking about what those seventh-grade girls had said that morning. *Bring back Jack?* Something about a poll on the *Bigwigs* forums? Hopefully it was just some dumb thing *Bigwigs* fans did to keep themselves busy while they waited for the next season to start. What would be the point of bringing old contestants back? Past winners, sure. Runners-up, maybe. But the rest? The ones who hadn't measured up? Why would anyone want to see *them* again?

After his Business and Enterprise elective, Jack bumped into Darylyn as they both headed for the quadrangle.

"So what are you thinking?" said Jack. "For next year's electives, I mean."

Darylyn raised her eyebrows. "Well, I don't want to startle you, Jack, but I think it's very likely that my subjects for next year will include math, computers . . . and computers."

"Right, of course," said Jack. "Computers. Good choice."

They walked the rest of the way to the quadrangle in silence. Reese and Vivi were already there by the time Jack and Darylyn arrived. The four of them had claimed one of the tables there halfway through seventh grade, and so far nobody had challenged them for it. Reese seemed especially psyched to see them—which made it all the more mysterious when he offered Jack a high five that was seriously lacking in swag. It was almost as though Reese had been looking right through him.

"So," said Jack. "Mayor for a Week. I told Vivi she should apply for it. She'd be a certainty, right?"

"Totally," said Reese.

Darylyn nodded. "To the extent that anything is certain, I would say hell yes."

Vivi shrugged. "I don't know. My grades haven't been so great this year. I probably don't need another distraction."

"What are you talking about?" said Jack. "You're still top of our class, last time I checked."

Vivi side-eyed him. "And you happen to know that because you're watching the competition, I guess?"

"Nerds," coughed Reese.

Vivi put on a shocked expression. "Nerds? I refute that statement most strenuously."

"As do I," said Jack. "Do you think we'd be sitting here at the cool table if we were nerds?"

"No," said Darylyn. "But let's face it—we're mostly here because of Reese's genetically acquired street cred."

Reese poked Darylyn in the arm and grinned. "That's racist."

This is new, thought Jack. Not the jesting, but the direct physical contact. Was this something male and female buddies did now? He waited a moment, then tentatively jabbed

Vivi in the arm. Unsure if he'd made a decisive enough jab, he did it again, harder.

"Ow! What the—?"

"Mayor for a Week," blurted Jack. "Are you going to do it or what?"

Vivi rubbed her arm and winced. "It depends. First of all, they might require a candidate with a full set of functioning limbs."

"Sorry," said Jack. "It's all this new muscle tone I've suddenly got. So annoying. I guess I don't know my own strength."

"Second," said Vivi, ignoring him, "since it's just a popularity contest, they'll probably end up giving it to someone like *her* again." She pointed at four eleventh graders cruising through the quadrangle as though it were a beachside esplanade.

Natsumi Distagio and the Shieling twins, thought Jack. As usual there was a random fourth member of the entourage—a budding beta-babe orbiting Nats's inner circle.

Reese leaned toward Jack. "Dude, is that your *sister*?"

Jack looked closer, then found himself nodding dumbly as he realized that, yes, apparently Hallie was now rolling with Upland's topmost division of divas. One more thing that seemed to have changed between the end of the first semester and the start of the second.

"Wow," said Vivi. "You could totally work that to your advantage, Jack. Marry into the Distagio family. Become an instant millionaire. Plus, she's so pretty."

Jack shrugged. "She's okay."

Okay, he thought. *Okay in the same way that flying in an F-35 stealth jet would be "okay."*

Natsumi Distagio's tan was just that shade more perfect than anyone else's. Her eyes, nose, and mouth were crucial millimeters closer to ideal. Her hair had optimum bounce and luster. Natsumi Distagio—and Jack felt this was no exaggeration—was a hottie of sufficient magnitude to be one of those models who stood at the back of the stage during the presentation of a People's Choice Award.

Vivi nudged Jack. "So when are you going to pop the question?"

"Huh? Why am *I* being singled out here? What about Reese? He's a guy. Like me. We're both guys. Both . . . fully grown guys."

Vivi glanced at Reese, who flinched at the sudden attention.

"Somehow I don't think Reese has his eye on Nats," said Vivi wryly. "Anyway, I think it's good you've got yourself a love interest."

Good in what way? wondered Jack. He felt it again—the feeling he'd been having the whole year, of some uncrossable gap between them, of being talked down to. When Vivi said it was "good," it sounded like the sort of "good" you'd say to a puppy who'd finally learned to poop in the right spot.

"Because it's such a joke that I could be with someone like her . . . ," he muttered.

"She *is* significantly older than you," Darylyn noted. "Though the age difference only seems so pronounced because of the wide variance of physical and emotional maturity in adolescent populations."

There was an awkward pause. Reese glanced from side to side, then hastily unwrapped the earbuds from his battered MP3 player. "So . . . I just found out about this thing called Calypso War. It's, like, these Caribbean singers in the fifties who went around dissing each other like total gangstas—"

Vivi poked Jack in the arm. "I didn't mean to make fun of you."

Jack shrugged. "Whatever."

"Actually, I *did* mean to make fun of you. But only in a 'we're all grown-ups and can look after ourselves' kind of way."

That's the problem, thought Jack. It didn't feel like that at all. It felt more like they were making fun of him in a "you can't possibly be our equal because it seems very doubtful that you possess any pubes yet" kind of way.

Chapter Four

~~~~~~

At no time was Jack more aware of the "wide variance of physical and emotional maturity in adolescent populations" than when he had his Monday afternoon double lesson of PE.

For a start, Mr. Delphi was the kind of PE teacher who didn't see any problem leaving it up to students to choose sides for team sports. Jack was a long way from being top pick, which was bad enough as weekly humiliation went. But that wasn't even the worst thing.

The worst thing was the locker room.

Jack was pretty sure Vivi and Darylyn and all the other girls got to disrobe in civilized silence behind their own personal bamboo screens, possibly with the sound of flutes piping into the locker room through a speaker somewhere. The boys' locker room, on the other hand, was basically an open-plan dungeon built for maximum psychological torture.

The building itself appeared to have needed repairs for decades. The floor was carpeted with a mulch of stray socks, the air was a haze of weird body odors and stale deodorant, and there were occasional random assessments of whose testicles had dropped and whose hadn't.

There was one other major difference between the girls' locker room and the boys' locker room.

The girls' locker room didn't have Oliver Sampson.

Oliver Sampson was in 8D, and his problem was the exact opposite of Jack's—if being rigged like a horse between your legs really qualified as a problem. Like Jack, Sampson had gone to elementary school at Upland West. And then, sometime between the end of sixth grade and the start of seventh, Sampson had been swept up in the biggest testosterone tsunami in recorded history. Over the course of a single summer break he'd tripled in size in every direction. When he'd stripped down in the locker room that first week of junior high, the other new seventh graders literally *cowered*, as if they'd received a visitation from some extraterrestrial superbeing. ("Who *is* this god who walks among us?" someone had whispered.)

But as the months passed, the rest of the boys cowered

no more as they inched toward the benchmark Sampson had set. Soon they were no longer boys, but fledgling dudes.

All except Jack. Even Kenny Hodgman—Jack's last ally in eighth-grade pubelessness—seemed to have betrayed him. Just since the end of first semester, the Hodgemeister's voice had dropped so far he sounded like Darth Vader to Jack's Jar Jar Binks.

Jack dumped his backpack on one of the benches farthest from Sampson and the others. He stood looking at it, contemplating how to get his school clothes off and his soccer shorts on before anyone noticed he'd finally become the only minnow in the shark tank.

"Hey, Jack!"

Jack looked up. It was Philo Dawson, Vivi's younger cousin. He zoomed toward Jack, shoulders jerking forward, as though his whole body were being reeled along by the semicrazed grin that seemed to leap a mile ahead of the rest of his face.

"Hey, Philo."

"Can you believe it's second semester already, Jack?" Philo shook his head wistfully. "Eighth grade, almost over."

Technically, Philo should have been looking forward to the end of seventh grade. He was a full year younger than Jack, but his parents had insisted he be pushed up a year so he could finish school sooner and take on his responsibilities to the family business: Raisin World.

It was wrinkled grapes that had put Upland on the map. Raisins had become such big business that a previous generation of Dawsons had built a Raisin World amusement park in the middle of Upland. They called it Raisin World World. So when Philo's parents had demanded that Philo—sole heir to the Raisin World empire—be allowed to skip a grade, the board of education had agreed. Partly because agreeing with Philo's side of the Dawson family was just what everyone in Upland did. But mostly because the sooner Philo finished school, the less likely he was to accidentally burn it down.

Philo unzipped his long, old-school gym bag and pulled out his soccer gear. "So how was your break, Jack?"

Jack was about to answer when he heard an unwelcome sound behind him: the many-octaves-too-low voice of Oliver Sampson.

"Yeah, Sprogless, how was your break?" Sampson loomed behind him, shirt off, chin raised, shoulders absurdly wide. "Didn't see you at the Under Fifteens sign-up." Being spoken at by Sampson was like the verbal equivalent of being jabbed in the ribs. "What happened? Finally get booted back to the Under Twelves where you belong?"

Jack was pretty sure the only kind of under-fifteens club *Sampson* deserved to join was a club for people with fifteen IQ points or under, but he didn't say this. He put on a disappointed face and shrugged. "I'll probably have to give baseball a miss this year. Got a bit of a . . . groin problem, actually."

"Groin problem?"

Jack bowed his legs and made a halfhearted pelvic thrust. In theory, it was meant to suggest a massive weight in the front part of his underpants. In practice, it looked like he'd suffered an accident in the back part.

Sampson snorted. "As if. Everyone knows you're a total baldy-balls."

The locker room turned into an echoing cavern of laughter. Only Philo and Kenny Hodgman remained silent. Sampson merged back into the mass of wide shoulders and underarm hair that was everyone else in the locker room who wasn't Jack Sprigley.

"He's such a bonehead," said Philo.

"Y-yeah," said Jack.

"I mean, he called you 'Sprogless,' and that's not even your name."

Jack grabbed his backpack and headed for the toilet cubicles next to the showers. Sampson had decided one thing for him, at least. There was no way he was going to get changed out in the open now.

"Where are you going?" asked Philo.

"Where does it look like I'm going?"

"But why are you taking all your stuff with you?"

"Oh," said Jack, glancing down at the open backpack. "Well, that's because . . . I've got these new Nikes? They're megaexpensive. Probably shouldn't let them out of my sight."

"Are you sure they're new? They look a little worn."

"That's . . . designer scuffing. It's the new thing."

"I can watch them for you if you're worried—"

"No, really, it's fine. I'll just take my gear in with me. Actually, since I'm doing the whole toilet thing anyway, maybe it'd be just as easy to get into my shorts and stuff while I'm in there."

"Okay," said Philo. "I just thought you might have been worried about the . . . you know. The *pubes* thing."

Jack snorted. "I'm not worried. Why would I be worried? Sampson doesn't know what he's talking about. I'm totally normal, pube-wise. I'm just the same as everyone else."

Just then, Jack caught a glimpse of Kenny Hodgman, who was doing his best to get his soccer shorts over the significant deposit the puberty fairy had recently paid into his underpants. Jack blinked in disbelief. It didn't seem possible that one person could need to grow *that* much genitalia in such a short space of time. Who needed to reproduce *that* urgently?

Philo waved a hand in front of Jack's face. "Are you okay, Jack?"

"Y-yep."

"You've gone a bit pale."

"I'm okay. I'll . . . I'll be out in a minute." Jack closed the cubicle door, dropped his backpack, and leaned against the wall.

He wasn't fooling anyone. Sampson saw right through him. Even Philo knew the score.

Which meant Vivi and Reese and Darylyn probably saw through him too.

The tide was rising on Pubeless Island.

The PE double turned out to be only marginally less humiliating than the locker room. After some warm-ups, half the kids Mr. Delphi had for PE that day were sent off to practice dribbling and passing, and the rest gathered at one of the soccer nets to choose sides for a game.

Jack hung at the back with Philo and Vivi as Mr. Delphi selected captains for each side.

"Oliver Sampson. Your turn again. And . . . let's see—"

Mr. Delphi's eyes roved closer and closer to where Jack stood with Vivi and Philo.

Not me, not me, not me, thought Jack. The last thing he wanted was to show the world how very far he and Sampson were from being equals.

"How about young Vivi Dink-Dawson?"

Jack breathed a sigh of relief as Vivi and Sampson stepped forward and took turns choosing their sides. Sampson's first pick was Tom Ziyadi—an instant expert at whatever sport you threw at him.

"Not the most imaginative choice," Mr. Delphi said.

Vivi's first pick was Jack.

Mr. Delphi raised his eyebrows. "Maybe a little *too* imaginative there, Dawson."

"Want to go goalie?" Vivi whispered, as Sampson made another predictably athletic choice for his second lieutenant.

"Sure," said Jack. For one thing, it spared him the embarrassment of rubbing shoulders (or not) with the other, more advanced, male specimens out on the field. He hoped that wasn't why Vivi had suggested it. He preferred to think of it as a vote of confidence: her way of saying she was happy for Jack to have her back.

Once the sides were picked, the players jogged out onto the field, leaving Jack alone in the goal square. For ten, then fifteen minutes, he watched the game play out in the distance. Jack didn't want to complain about his team's unexpected prowess against Sampson's pack of supermen, but he was starting to get bored. He was just wondering if he'd ever get involved in the action when Sampson suddenly burst free from a misjudged tackle from Philo and streaked out in front of the rest of the field. Startled, Jack inched forward, trying to guess which way Sampson would strike.

Sampson locked eyes with Jack—and shot for goal.

Jack made a desperate lunge toward the ball, but he couldn't get his hands to it in time. The shot went right through his defenses.

A whistle blew. There were muted grunts of victory from out on the field, as though the result had never been in doubt. Sampson threw a look over his shoulder.

"You could've saved that if you were bigger, Sprigley."

The match finished one–nil. One winner.

And one loser.

Chapter Five

~~~~~~

Square jaw. Bulging biceps. Rippling abs.

"Need help?" asked the pharmacist's assistant. She chewed her gum at Jack and blinked.

Jack backed away from the shelf of protein powder cans. "No, I was just . . ." The row of identically muscular titans on the labels of the cans glowered back at him. Jack turned away from them and rolled his eyes at the assistant. "Wow. What sort of loser would buy this stuff?"

"You have to be fourteen or older," said the assistant. "Sorry."

"I *am* fourteen," said Jack.

The assistant raised her eyebrows. "Really?"

Jack sighed and handed over the prescription. "I need to pick this up for my gran," he said. He felt waves of testosterone emanating from the wall of protein powder. Oliver Sampson's taunt played over and over in his head.

"You could've saved that if you were bigger."

Well, he *had* been bigger, once upon a time. He'd been a bigger deal than anyone at Upland West or Upland Junior High. But now he'd stepped so far out of the spotlight that no one even seemed to remember that anymore.

Jack followed the assistant over to the counter. "I used to be on TV," he heard himself say.

The pharmacist's assistant looked up at him, blank-faced. "My second cousin was in an ad for Raisin World when she was in second grade. She got paid, like, two hundred dollars."

Jack looked apologetic. "Um, my thing was kind of a bigger deal than an ad for Raisin World, actually."

"Avocado World? That is a pretty big deal, I guess." She handed Jack a white paper bag.

Jack pulled out the fifty-dollar bill his gran had given him that morning. "Ten thousand dollars. That's how much I won."

The assistant stopped chewing her gum. "Wow. You could buy our entire shelf of muscle powder with that."

Jack headed straight for his gran's bungalow when he got home.

Jack's gran, Marlene, had moved into the bungalow behind the house two years ago. Her unit on the other side of Upland had been slowly falling to pieces ever since Jack's step-granddad, Clive, had run off with all of Marlene's savings. Jack had wanted to do something useful with his *Bigwigs* winnings (or "losings," as he called them), so he'd put the prize money toward renovating the bungalow for his gran to live in. For a while there, he'd felt like he was doing his bit. Like he really was the man of the house.

"Knock, knock," he shouted. He waited a moment, then pushed open the door.

Marlene was lounging on her bed, an old-generation iPhone with a turquoise case in one hand and a clunky gray dumbphone resting on the bedspread next to her.

Hallie had handed the iPhone down to her a few weeks ago. "Just because I don't have thousands of dollars to give away," she'd said, "doesn't mean I can't be generous if I want to."

Marlene squinted at one phone and then the other through her glasses. The radio (loud) and TV (muted) were both playing in the background.

"Gran?"

Marlene looked up. "Jack!" She tossed the iPhone aside as though she'd been caught shoplifting. "Home already? Gosh, time flies."

"I've got your stuff from the pharmacy," he said, handing

her the white paper bag. "Is everything okay with the phone?"

"What phone, dear?"

Jack paused. "Hallie's old phone. The one you *just* had in your hand."

"Oh!" said Marlene, glancing down at the iPhone in surprise. "Yes. I've just been copying my numbers over."

"Do you need a hand—?"

"No," said Marlene sharply. "No, I'll manage, dear. Thank you."

Jack felt his phone buzz in his pocket. The noise sent Marlene lunging for the iPhone she'd just tossed aside.

"Um, I think that was me," said Jack.

"Right," said Marlene, nodding casually and edging back across the bed. "Good-o."

Jack's phone buzzed a second time. Marlene eyed the iPhone on the bed nervously.

"I guess I'll find out who that is," said Jack.

"What?" said Marlene, ashen-faced.

"I mean, I'll . . . find out who's texting me."

"Oh," said Marlene. "Yes, that's a better idea."

Jack turned to leave, but found himself lingering at the doorway.

"Wait," he said, turning around. "So what did you—?"

Marlene quickly crossed her arms and jammed the iPhone—which she appeared to have picked up again the moment Jack had turned his back—into her left armpit. "What now?"

Jack paused. "Never mind."

Jack dumped his backpack by the kitchen door, grabbed a Raisin World grape juice from the fridge, then checked the messages on his phone.

It was Vivi who'd texted him.

Where were u after school? said the first text.

U didn't wait for us, said the second.

Jack turned his phone off and went to grab his laptop from his backpack. Of course he hadn't waited. Why remind them yet again of the several anatomically significant reasons why he completely failed to fit in with them anymore?

And anyway, there was somewhere else he'd decided he needed to be. A place he'd never dared go before.

Jack put his laptop on the kitchen bench. He opened a new browser window and navigated to the page he wanted, wondering if this was really a good idea.

Before he knew it, his fingers were on the keyboard. He glanced at his switched-off phone, took a deep breath, and typed three words:

Bring back Jack.

Chapter Six

~~~~~~

"We think Jack stands a very good chance of getting onto the program," Ms. Aria said to Jack's mom. "He's got a lot of charisma. He's very popular here at Upland West. And he's clever, obviously. He has an excellent head for solving problems within a team and bringing out the best in others." Ms. Aria smiled. "I really do think this would be a terrific opportunity for him."

Ms. Aria opened up her laptop and played a clip from a mock quiz show they'd filmed during the school camp the year before. "Remember this, Jack?"

"Yes, Ms. Aria."

"Jack played the quizmaster," Ms. Aria explained. "You can

see what a natural he is. The producers have been asking local schools to suggest candidates who tick all the boxes, who might be good ambassadors for Upland. They're looking for someone quick-thinking as well as someone who shines on camera. We think Jack's a good bet."

Jack's mom leaned forward in her chair, leafing through the forms. Her eyes flicked up and down each page. It was a relief for Jack to see something other than an abandoned, empty look in her eyes. She glanced up at him. "What do you think, Jack?"

"It sounds . . . totally awesome," said Jack, trying to appear enthusiastic. It hadn't been his first thought, when Ms. Aria had started talking about this Bigwigs thing. But he would've done or said anything to keep that sad look from his mom's face.

Jack turned to Ms. Aria. "Is there prize money?"

His mom looked embarrassed. "Don't do it for money, Jack! We're not that desperate!"

"There's prize money for the finalists, yes," said Ms. Aria. "But I think it's the experience—the opportunity to use your talents—that you'll find most rewarding. It's a competition, there's no denying that, but I think you'll find it's best not to focus on that side of things."

Adele nodded. "I'll be proud of you no matter how far you get. And . . . your dad would have said the same."

Even after three years, Jack still wasn't used to hearing "your dad" in the past tense. He looked at Ms. Aria. "Everyone would still *treat me like normal, right? It wouldn't be . . . weird afterward?"*

"People might treat you a little differently at first," said Ms. Aria. "But of anyone in our sixth-grade group, Jack, you're the one I think is most likely to handle whatever . . . recognition might come from being on the program."

"You mean, he's not some ego-crazed maniac," said Adele.

Ms. Aria smiled. "Jack is definitely not an ego-crazed maniac, no."

Jack took a swig from his Raisin World juice and scanned the search results.

Even as a contestant he'd fought the urge to take a peek at the *Bigwigs* forums. He remembered Mickey Santini having some sort of mini nervous breakdown after reading what the fans had said about his "make it up as you go along" approach to the week three pet food commercial challenge, when Yellow Team had been sent to work at the Normington-Price advertising agency. Jack mentally high-fived his sixth-grade self for exercising superior self-restraint.

It didn't take him long to find what he was looking for.

Me and my friends go to school with Jack Sprigley and he's super hot! wrote ^kitty^cat on the "Next Season News" thread. Nobody knows anything about him and he's all mysterious. Not like Piers Blain, who's in all the magazines all the time. Boring! BRING BACK JACK!

Jack had never thought of himself as mysterious. It wasn't like he'd been deliberately secretive or enigmatic or anything. Sometimes you just couldn't control how other people saw you.

BRING BACK JACK! wrote {e-girrl}. Piers Blain is boring and also gross. He has little bits of hair in his armpits and even some on his chest. O__o.

Immediately after that, Urchn weighed in.

Yeah, we like Jack because he's super huggy and you could have him for a sleepover and not have to worry because he's like a little teddy bear or something. But not hairy like a teddy bear. Not hairy at all! BRING BACK JACK!

Jack nearly spat out his juice. He was about to close the laptop when the title of one of the other forum posts caught his eye.

Reality TV Champion Blain Scores $1M Luxury Apartment

One of the forum members—obviously more of a fan of Piers Blain than ^kitty^cat, {e-girrl}, or Urchn—had posted a link to a recent news article.

Former *Bigwigs* star Piers Blain spent his break approving the finishing touches on a harbor-side apartment, which he'll take occupancy of next month.

"The main thing was fine-tuning the self-dimming lights in the Xbox room," said Blain, fourteen. "And choosing the right beanbags. These ones are designed by the team that built Lady Gaga's robotic third arm."

Blain will have his own live-in chaperone and tutor, and has said he intends to "party responsibly" while also focusing on "blitzing" his final few years of high school, reviewing games for the Byteface video blog, and continuing his appearances as the public face of the "Be Cool to Each Other" anti-bullying campaign.

Jack had seen the anti-bullying ads. "Being a bully doesn't make you a big person," Piers said earnestly into the camera. "Being a big person means having a big responsibility. A responsibility to be *awesome*."

The only time Jack had ever been the public face of anything was just before the start of junior high school, when he was invited to open the Upland South Childcare Center alongside the town's sixty-year-old bachelor mayor, Neville Perry-Moore. (The newspaper headline: CARING FOR TOMORROW'S BIGWIGS.) His mom and his gran had come along as well, and the whole thing had just felt massively dumb and awkward. Jack couldn't imagine doing that kind of thing week in, week out, the way Piers Blain seemed to. Maybe that was why Piers Blain had his own apartment and Jack didn't.

Since when did fourteen-year-olds acquire patches of prime beachfront real estate, anyway? It was hard enough growing a visible patch of *pubic hair*.

Jack wondered if any of the other ex-Bigwigs who'd found fame and fortune had even *tried* to go back to a normal life again. Maybe trying to be normal, like Jack had done, was the total opposite of normal.

He closed the laptop. He was none the wiser about this "bringing back past contestants" thing. Which, if he was honest, was kind of a relief. As small as he felt now, going anywhere near *Bigwigs* again was guaranteed to make him feel even smaller.

"Jack, you're home."

Jack looked up and saw his mom stepping over his backpack. She usually came home for a few hours in the afternoon before heading off to the golf club to set up for some party or event. She dumped her handbag on the bench, spilling keys, tissues, mints, and loyalty cards everywhere.

"Hi, Mom." Jack drummed his fingers on the laptop. "Weird question, but you'd tell me if the *Bigwigs* people had been in touch, right?"

Adele opened the fridge and reached into the crisper for an apple. "*Bigwigs*? Of course. Why? Is there extra prize money they forgot to give us? Please let it be that."

"Doesn't matter."

"Speaking of money, I saw your sister down the street. Looks like she's started hanging out with one of Bruno Distagio's girls."

"I know," said Jack.

Adele bit into the apple. "You could marry into the family and make us rich."

Jack's hand tightened around the empty juice bottle. "Why does everyone think that's so goddamn *funny?*"

Adele paused, then shut the fridge door. "It wasn't meant to be—Jack, is something the matter?"

"Oh, nothing." He slammed the Raisin World bottle down on the bench and crossed his arms. "Obviously it's just *hilarious* that I'm the smallest guy in eighth grade—and everyone knows it. Do you realize how much of a *loser* that makes me? Half of the eighth-grade guys look like freaking *lumberjacks.*"

"You're not a loser, Jack."

"Well, I lost *Bigwigs*, didn't I? And now I'm losing at everything else."

His mom frowned at him. "Is that really what you think?" she said quietly. "That you *lost Bigwigs?*"

"It doesn't matter," Jack muttered.

"This isn't why you were avoiding Vivi and the others over the break, is it?"

"I wasn't avoiding them. They were avoiding *me.*"

"I'm sure they weren't."

Jack gave her a look.

"Well, if you really want to show everyone how mature

you are, just let them know how you're feeling. There's noth-ing more grown-up than that."

Easier said than done, thought Jack. Hallie was the only one in the Sprigley household who seemed okay with tell-ing everyone how she was feeling—but hers was more of a megaphone-and-skywriting approach, which was just as bad.

His mom must have noticed the skeptical look on his face. "All I'm saying is, it's got to be better than getting your-self into a panic and assuming the worst."

"Uh-huh," said Jack. His mom didn't get it. He'd already spent the first day back at school trying to convince everyone he was a fully paid-up member of the reproductive organs brigade. He couldn't just confess that he'd committed per-jury with respect to the status of his pubes.

And anyway, he was pretty sure that real men didn't take advice from their moms. If a real man needed advice, he'd get it from a manlier source. He'd get it from . . . well, a man.

Or at least someone who was considerably closer to being a man than Jack could claim to be.

Chapter Seven

~~~~~~

Jack got up early to take a detour to Reese's house before school.

It was more a fact-finding mission than anything else. Jack had almost convinced himself he'd missed some kind of secret initiation ceremony into the world of pubes. Maybe it was something as simple as knowing which brand of undies to wear to bed. Maybe you weren't supposed to wear undies at all. Or maybe it was a chicken-and-egg situation, and he wasn't trying hard enough with the whole masturbation thing.

Yes, that's a great idea, thought Jack. *I'm sure Reese would not be at all fazed if I ask him for a one-on-one MASTURBATION tutorial.* (*Dude,* Jack imagined him saying, *you should not need to use two hands.*)

Obviously he wouldn't take it that far. Just a few well-placed questions, and a bit of low-key, information-based male bonding. And maybe, if it happened to come up in conversation, he could subtly seek Reese's reassurance that he was still part of the gang and not just a pathetic hanger-on.

The spring breeze made the flowering bushes near the sidewalk sway like hula dancers as Jack turned the corner into Peppertree Drive. He was only a few steps down the road when he saw Reese vault one-handed over the low gate at the end of his driveway onto the sidewalk.

Jack checked his watch. Eight fifteen a.m. *Kind of early to be leaving for school,* he thought.

One of Reese's earbuds had popped out in the jump over the gate. Jack went to call out, hoping to get Reese's attention before he put the earbud back in, when he noticed someone waving at Reese from the other side of the street.

It was Darylyn.

Without knowing exactly why, Jack instinctively slunk back the way he'd come. Darylyn hadn't seen him yet. In fact, as she and Reese stared at each other across the street, they seemed to be suspended in a world of their own.

Jack ducked back behind the crooked wooden fence that ran alongside the house on the corner of the street. He watched as Darylyn checked for traffic. It was almost like they were doing a drugs drop-off or something.

Darylyn crossed the street to where Reese was waiting for her, holding out the spare earbud. And Darylyn *smiled*. Jack couldn't believe it. It was basically like looking at a completely different person. Then this quasi-imposter version of Darylyn let herself be joined to Reese via earbud cable, and together they walked to school.

Jack crept out from behind the fence. It wasn't a drugs drop-off, he realized grimly. *What it looks like,* thought Jack, *is a lovey-dovey drop-in.*

He took a few steps after his friends, then saw Reese reach for Darylyn's hand.

Then Darylyn reached for Reese's hand. Their hands touched, and the two of them leaned in toward each other—

And then, at the last moment, Reese stopped, as if he'd sensed something. He turned to look over his shoulder. . . .

And that was when Jack—quick-thinking, problem-solving, reality-TV-show contestant Jack Sprigley—made the split-second decision to dive into a lavender bush.

Chapter Eight

Jack waited outside his classroom for first period alone.

Reese and Darylyn had apparently been so caught up in their private hand-holding, earbud-sharing love-zone that they hadn't even waited at the school gate for him.

Meanwhile, Vivi had been a no-show in homeroom that morning.

Where are you? Jack texted. He switched his phone off silent so he'd be sure to get her reply as soon as she sent it.

How long has this Reese and Darylyn thing been going on? he wondered. They'd been friends since elementary school, before Jack even knew them, so it wasn't weird that they'd walked to school together. But the hand-holding and the almost-kissing was definitely weird.

He wondered if Vivi knew. Maybe she did. Maybe Jack was doomed to be the last one to find out—possibly because he'd been the last one to join the gang, but more likely because he was the only one who hadn't sprouted functioning sex parts yet.

The rest of 8C milled about the hallway. Jack picked out some of the faces he'd known since Upland West Elementary: people he'd sat next to in class, people he'd played sports with, people he'd been *friends* with, even. But then there'd been *Bigwigs*, and the start of junior high, and meeting Vivi and Reese and Darylyn. Everyone had outgrown the old bonds from elementary school.

He wondered if he'd made a terrible mistake, turning away from his *Bigwigs* semifame. He should have cashed it in as a kind of popularity insurance policy. Maybe then it wouldn't have been so easy for everyone to leave him behind. As it was, he felt like an embarrassing leftover from another time.

A time before pubes.

"Jack!" said a voice behind him. Jack turned to see Philo standing in the hallway, grinning eagerly. "Hi! You've got lavender in your hair!"

Jack tipped his head forward and finger-combed the

purple flowers out of his bangs. "Hi, Philo."

"Speaking of hair . . ." Philo reached into his satchel.

Jack glanced at Philo warily. Speaking of *hair*? This did not sound good.

"That's right: I think I might have the solution to your problem!"

Jack shook his head. "I don't have a—"

"Ta-da!"

Philo handed Jack a flap of beige-colored cloth with a dense mass of black, wiry strands stitched to it. Underneath the cloth were several strips of carefully positioned double-sided tape.

Jack stared at it for a moment. Then he stared at it a moment longer.

"Is this what I think it is?" he whispered, wide-eyed with horror. He looked up at Philo in a panic. "Is this . . . holy crap, is this a *merkin*?"

"I don't know," Philo whispered back. "What's a merkin?"

Jack took Philo aside and shook the wiry thatch at him. "It's this!" he hissed, keeping his voice low so no one else would hear. "It's what *this* is. *This* is a merkin. This *pube wig* is a merkin!"

In seventh grade, Jack had mistyped the word "Merlin" in an English essay and became curious when the spell-checker didn't pick it up. One image search later, and a whole new world of pubic fashion had been laid bare—or not—before him.

"Oh," said Philo, looking annoyed. "I didn't realize that was already a thing."

"You mean . . . you came up with the idea of a merkin *by yourself?*"

"Yeah, I guess so. Wow, now I feel stupid. I could've just bought one on the Internet or something. Anyway, it's just so you don't have to feel so out of place in the locker room."

"No, this wouldn't make me look out of place *at all*," Jack said, rolling his eyes. Then he stopped. "Wait, if you didn't *buy* this . . ."

"I made it."

"You *made* it?"

"With Mother's sewing kit. It took me all night."

Jack turned the material over in his hands. Gross and creepy though it was, he had to admit Philo had put a lot of effort into it. "You know, it's actually pretty solid work. . . . What did you use for the—?" Then his eyes widened. "Wait . . . Oh my God, it's not *your* hair, is it?"

Philo went suddenly shifty-eyed. "What?"

Jack held the homemade merkin as far away as possible without attracting attention from the rest of the class down the hallway. "Have you just given me a handful of *your own pubes?*" he hissed.

"Would that be bad?"

"Yes, that would be bad!"

"Even if they'd been shampooed first?"

Jack's eyes widened even further. "So they *are* your pubes!"

Philo paused. "I didn't say that."

"Whose are they, then?"

"Whose are what?"

"Whose *pubes* are they? What else would I be talking about when I'm *holding a bunch of pubes*? What were you expecting me to *do* with this thing, anyway?" Jack whispered. "*Wear* it?"

"Just until . . ." Philo lowered his hands and made wafting motions upward in an apparent attempt to mime the growth of pubic hair.

"I don't believe this!"

"You'd be more like Oliver Sampson," said Philo.

"Why? Does he have someone else's pubes stuffed down his jocks as well?"

"Sampson? I don't know. You could ask him!"

"Ask me what?"

Jack turned to see Sampson standing behind him. And standing next to Sampson was homeroom no-show and recent nonreplier-to-texts, Vivi Dink-Dawson.

"Hey, Cuz," she said to Philo. "Hey, Jack." She tried to see what Jack was holding. "Oh my God, what is that?"

"Nothing," said Jack, stuffing the merkin into his pocket. "And Philo was just leaving. Weren't you, Philo?"

"I sure was!" said Philo. "If I don't get a move on, I'll be late for school!"

Sampson frowned. "You're . . . at school already?"

Philo blinked. "Okay, that was pretty stupid, even for me. I guess I shouldn't have stayed up so late making Jack that merk—"

"Merkel!" blurted Jack. "That . . . sculpture of Angela Merkel. You know. The German prime minister or whatever. Oh man, she's definitely my favorite world leader who's a lady."

Philo now looked even more confused than normal. Jack gave him a little shove to send him on his way, then turned back to Vivi.

Sampson was still hovering next to her. It was almost as though Vivi had temporarily forgotten what a massive brainless jerk he was.

"I thought you must have been sick or something," said Jack, doing his best to ignore Sampson. "I mean, that Mayor for a Week thing is on today, right? I didn't think you'd want to miss that."

"I think you'll find Angela Merkel is the German *chancellor*," said Sampson, "not prime minister."

"Oh," said Jack. "Really?"

Really? he thought. *Sampson knows a three-syllable word?*

"That's why we're late," said Vivi. "We bumped into each other at the bus stop and just got fully into this conversation about whether I should apply or not. Oliver's coming to the information session too."

"We got talking yesterday after PE," Sampson explained. He glanced down at Vivi. "You know, comparing notes on the soccer match. One captain to another!"

"A meeting of equals!" joked Vivi.

Jack looked from Vivi to Sampson and back again. What the hell was going on? "I . . . thought we'd already agreed you should definitely go for it?" he said.

Vivi frowned. "I don't think we had. Anyway, I figured it couldn't hurt to get another opinion. Mix things up a little."

Jack couldn't help thinking things seemed plenty mixed-up already.

"Oliver's going to meet me outside the student center, before the information session." Vivi caught Jack's eye. "I thought you'd probably want to tag along too?"

"Yeah," said Jack. "Sure." What could he do: Say no? Risk getting on Vivi's bad side? It wasn't an option. Not with Sampson looking very much on her *good* side. "Tag along. That sounds like my kind of thing. . . ."

Vivi brightened. "Awesome! I already have some ideas about what I'd like to do as Mayor for a Week—"

(This came as no surprise to Jack.)

"—but I was thinking you guys could help me out, maybe workshop some stuff, kick some other ideas around?"

"Totally," said Jack. "I'm actually pretty good with that sort of thing." He glanced up at Sampson, suddenly feeling as though he was on surer ground. "You know, from being on *Bigwigs*. When you think about it, it's pretty similar. Kids doing adult jobs. And *Bigwigs* was a competition, Mayor for a Week's a competition . . . So, yeah—I'm *totally* qualified to help."

"*Bigwigs,*" Sampson snorted. "Like anyone watches that show anymore. Just because it's moved to network TV and it's running in prime time and has brand-new corporate sponsors and bigger prizes and . . ." He stopped, seeming to notice the way Vivi and Jack were looking at him. "I mean, I don't really keep up with it. That's just what I heard. All I'm saying is, it's still a stupid kids' show."

The bell rang for first period.

"So we'll see you later, yeah?" said Vivi, looking at Sampson.

"Totes," said Sampson. He flashed a dark look at Jack, which went unnoticed by Vivi, then walked off down the hall.

"What are you doing getting *him* involved in this?" hissed Jack.

"In what?" said Vivi.

"In this! In . . . *us*."

"I . . . don't think there *is* an 'us,' Jack."

"Not *us* us. I mean all of us. Me and you and Reese and Darylyn." Again, Jack wondered if Vivi knew about Reese and Darylyn's secret pairing. If she did, she didn't show it.

"Look, Jack," said Vivi, "things aren't always going to stay the same . . ."

(Jack wanted to mention that he had two semesters' worth of looking down his pajama bottoms that suggested otherwise.)

". . . and anyway, Oliver actually seems like an okay guy when you get to know him. Plus, the only reason we got talking yesterday after PE was because you disappeared on me."

Disappeared, thought Jack. That's exactly what he felt was happening. He wondered how long it would be before nobody saw him at all.

Chapter Nine

he tables in the student center had been cleared to one side. Jack counted about twenty seventh and eighth graders sitting in two half-circle rows of chairs facing the guest speaker from Upland City Council. Jack deliberately sat in the row behind Vivi and Sampson, so he could eavesdrop on them without drawing attention to himself.

He wasn't sure what he expected to hear. Some accidental confession? Some careless hint confirming his suspicion that they'd become an oddly matched romantic couple overnight? (*King Kong and the lady from* King Kong, thought Jack.)

All that actually happened was that for the whole first

ten minutes of the session, Jack kept having to lean from side to side to see past Sampson's oxlike shoulders.

The other kids in the room were the junior high's best and brightest: the high achievers, the popular kids, the all-arounders, the online-petition makers and rally marchers. For a moment Jack was reminded of the cast meetings for *Bigwigs*, when the contestants would all be crammed into a dingy production office and briefed on their workplace challenge for the week. An office like the one where Jack had been told the real reason he wouldn't be making it any further in the finals.

"We're looking for someone with the maturity to represent their school in the community," the woman from the mayor's office was saying, "but also someone who can learn from having the town's top job for a week. If you think that person is you, I'd encourage you to find someone to nominate you and choose one of the essay topics listed on the application form. And I think that's all I need to tell you, except to say: good luck!"

Jack and Vivi's homeroom teacher, Mr. Jacobs, led the assembled students in applause.

Vivi turn to Sampson. "Essay topics?" Jack heard her say. She looked confused, as though she couldn't work out whether to be annoyed or not. "They must have changed the rules. I guess it's not just a popularity contest after all."

Meanwhile, the junior high dean of students, Ms. Liaw, had stepped off into one of the offices adjoining the student center to fetch the next speaker. It hadn't even occurred to Jack who it would be, but suddenly there she was: Nats Distagio.

There were murmurings of disapproval from some of the seventh and eighth graders. Jack half expected Vivi to turn around and make another joke about him marrying into the Distagio family. He almost wished she would. Any attention would be better than no attention at all.

Nats glanced quickly down at the index cards in her hand, cleared her throat, then straightened her back and lifted her chin. "Imagine being able to walk a week in someone else's shoes. To see the big picture." She gazed earnestly at the assembled seventh and eighth graders. "Imagine being given the opportunity to bring people together. To make a differ-ence. That's what it felt like the week I was Mayor for a Week. It's an experience I'll always remember—even in five years' time when I've got my dream job as a prime-time TV host."

More murmurings.

Nats moved to the next card and glanced up again. "I can see many familiar faces here today—"

Jack felt a hot prickling sensation creep up his neck. It suddenly occurred to him: Maybe Nats had watched *Bigwigs*. Maybe she recognized him from TV. Maybe she knew who he was.

"—and I'm sure every one of you would be a great ambassador for the school. Of course, it's not just what's underneath that counts. The Mayor for a Week is the public face of Upland. For a week. That face is somewhere in this room. That face could be your face. For a week."

Nats was moving on to her next card when Jack's phone buzzed and beeped in his pocket.

Crap, he thought. He'd stupidly forgotten to switch it back to silent from before, when he'd been waiting for Vivi to text him back.

Worse, it wasn't just a message. Someone was trying to call him.

He plunged his hand into his pocket to silence the phone—and frowned. He didn't remember packing a hankie in his pocket. And also, why was it covered in hairs?

His eyes widened. Philo's little homework project. Jack had jammed it into his pocket to hide it from Vivi and Sampson. It had been there ever since. A ticking time bomb of Philo Dawson's pubes.

And he'd just put his hand right onto it.

Ms. Liaw's gaze swept around the student center. "Whose phone is that?"

People started shifting in their chairs and craning their necks.

"Turn it off *now* unless you want it confiscated."

Jack's phone was ringing properly now. Loudly. He reached farther into his pocket, doing his best to avoid any contact with the merkin.

"Come on," said Mr. Jacobs. "Natsumi has taken time out from her classes to speak to you all. Show some respect."

The kids in the audience started looking in Jack's direction. Jack sat dead still, eyes straight ahead. He fumbled for the ringer toggle on the phone—and felt the adhesive kiss of double-sided tape against the back of his hand.

Goddamn it, thought Jack. He gave up trying to silence the phone. Instead he waggled his hand in his pocket, trying to shake Philo's homemade pube wig free.

Ms. Liaw craned her neck. "Jack? Is that your phone?"

The more Jack shook his hand, the tighter the merkin clung to it. "Er—"

"Jack Sprigley," said Mr. Jacobs. "You know better than this. Hand it over."

Everyone in the student center swung around to face him. Vivi and Sampson stared at him like he was crazy.

"Jack!" hissed Vivi. "Turn it off!"

The phone continued to ring. Jack couldn't pull out his hand without revealing the merkin. One glimpse of the pube wig and everyone would a) know for sure that Jack had no pubes of his own, and b) think he was a total freaking *weirdo.*
"Er—"

Mr. Jacobs snapped his fingers. *"Give it to me."*

He shook his hand in his pocket again, but the merkin was fully stuck to him. (Jack cursed Philo's excellent workmanship—and then changed his mind and cursed the fact that Philo had given him a pube wig *at all*.)

"What *is* going on in that pocket, Jack?" said Ms. Liaw, looking very concerned all of a sudden.

"Nothing, miss," said Jack, trying to keep his voice level.

"Then hurry up and *give me the phone*!"

"Miss, he's not getting his phone," someone said. "He's *inappropriately touching himself*!"

"What?" cried Jack. "No! I—"

Jack saw Vivi pull away from him in horror. A look of disgust spread across Ms. Liaw's face. Mr. Jacobs glanced from side to side, as if searching for a fire alarm to smash open. The woman from the council sat frozen, mouth agape. Nats took an involuntary step back and held her index cards up to her face.

Sampson leaped to his feet and held his hands out either side of him, like he was protecting the room from an escaped animal. "Stand back, everyone! Someone has obviously gotten a little bit excited." He looked scathingly at Jack. "And I do mean a *little* bit."

"No . . . ," Jack pleaded, his voice a hoarse, horrified whisper. He glanced at Vivi in desperation, nodding furiously toward the pocket his hand was still lodged in. "Sticky—"

"Oh my God," said Vivi, covering her mouth.

At that point, the woman from the council actually stood up on her chair, as if a mouse had run into the room.

Jack shook his hand in his pocket again, a pained expression on his face. "Sticky—"

His brain sent his mouth an urgent memo to stop using the word "sticky." But by then it was too late.

Far, far too late.

Chapter Ten

~~~~~~

"Ah, Sprigley. I've been looking through your file."

Mr. Trench was Upland Junior High's vice principal and student counselor. Before coming to work at the school, he'd been in the army reserve. Jack secretly doubted that Mr. Trench was trained in anything even resembling twenty-first-century counseling techniques. The only techniques he seemed to be trained in were techniques for exploding things at various distances.

"Close the door and sit down."

Jack had never been in this kind of trouble before. He sat down in the chair opposite Mr. Trench before his legs turned to soup beneath him.

"Now," said Mr. Trench, looking up from his desk. "I gather you've been caught abusing yourself in the student center."

Jack felt his face burn red with embarrassment. "No!"

"Well, obviously you *were* caught, or you wouldn't be here."

"But I wasn't *abusing* myself!"

"Wasn't abusing myself, *sir*," said Mr. Trench. "The point is, Sprigley, you were doing *something*—and doing it quite vigorously, as I understand it."

Jack felt sick. Vivi. Sampson. *Nats.* They'd all seen it. "No, *sir*. I definitely wasn't."

"Mr. Jacobs and Ms. Liaw seem pretty certain you were. Mrs. Hogarth was so disturbed by the news she's been forced to relocate her lunchtime Zumba class."

Jack couldn't stand it anymore. "Sir, I swear, nothing happened. The truth is . . . nothing *could* have happened."

Mr. Trench fixed his gaze on him. "Explain."

Jack hesitated, wondering exactly how he was going to communicate his embarrassing private details to a man who was so prehistoric that he probably thought women shouldn't be allowed to drive cars.

Jack swallowed. "Well, sir . . . the thing is, physically, I haven't actually . . . got that far. You know, down below."

Mr. Trench seemed genuinely confused. His fuzzy

eyebrows bunched together. "But you've got all the right arsenal, haven't you?"

Jack paused. He wasn't totally on board with the increasingly personal and military-themed direction in which the conversation was headed.

"Now, don't be coy," said Mr. Trench. "It's a sign of maturity to talk about these matters openly and honestly."

Or at least in army metaphors, thought Jack. He struggled to think of something to say, some answer that wouldn't be horribly embarrassing—but Mr. Trench had already picked up the phone.

"Bear with me, Sprigley, I'm going to have to call in reinforcements on this one."

Reinforcements? thought Jack.

"Hello? Yes, it's Rodney Trench here. I've got Jack Sprigley from eighth grade with me. Have I come through to Ms. Porter?"

Jack buried his head in his hands. Ms. Porter had started at the school at the beginning of the year. Unlike the previous Health Ed teacher, she was young enough to potentially remember what sex was actually like. Which meant there was at least one desperate attempt each class from one or another of the eighth-grade boys to get her to supply anecdotes from her own personal history.

"Right," said Mr. Trench, speaking into the phone. "Well,

I wonder if you might help me clarify something. It's concerning the physical development of the typical adolescent male."

Jack barely registered what Mr. Trench was saying as he discussed the ins and outs (mostly outs) of what was normal for a fourteen-year-old boy. He stopped listening altogether after he heard the words "Sprigley here insists he's totally lacking in ammunition."

"I see," said Mr. Trench, nodding thoughtfully. "Thank you." He put the phone down and turned to Jack. "Well, then. According to the intelligence I've just received, there are two commonly accepted markers that indicate whether a boy is, in fact, on the path to being a man. One: The testicles begin to enlarge. Two: The target acquires what's known as 'pubic hair.'" He paused. "So. Sprigley. Any testicular enlargement to report? Any 'pubic hair' on the radar?"

"Negative, sir. I mean, *no*. Sir."

"Well, let's not abandon hope. You're sure to experience the opening salvos of 'Operation: Manhood' sooner or later."

"Well, if Ms. Porter says so."

"Ms. Porter? No, she wasn't available as it happens."

Jack frowned. "Then . . . who were you talking to just now?"

"Good question. I could hear some vacuuming going on in the background, so it might have been one of the cleaners."

So it's worse than my private business being discussed with the Sex Ed teacher, thought Jack. *It's being discussed with the cleaning staff.* The younger of whom, according to Jack's sister, Hallie, sometimes bought alcohol for the eleventh graders and hung out with the twelfth graders, trading school gossip.

Mr. Trench regarded Jack for a moment. "I can see you're concerned, Sprigley. And perhaps quite rightly. So what if I were to suggest something that might help you advance the front line, so to speak?"

Jack had a feeling things were about to get even weirder.

"Manhood, you see, is not something that just *happens.* It's something that has to be taken charge of. There's a whole army of male sex hormones lying idle within you, Sprigley. An undisciplined rabble just waiting for a general to marshal them into action. It's *you* who must lead the charge. You must *act* like a man in order to *become* a man." Mr. Trench peered over his glasses at the papers on his desk. He picked them up and shuffled them nervously for a moment. "Now, I see from your file that you might be . . . well, let's say, 'lacking a strong male influence.' Your father, I gather he—?"

"Yeah," said Jack. "When I was nine."

There was silence for a moment. "And . . . what did he do?" Mr. Trench looked down at the paper again. "'Peter.'"

"He did the weather report on the local news," said Jack.

Mr. Trench frowned. Jack couldn't tell if he was trying to offer sympathy, or if he was just disappointed that Jack's dad hadn't been a policeman or firefighter or a tank commander or something.

When he was very young, Jack thought his dad actually *controlled* the weather—that the forecast he read out at the end of the news each night was a heavenly pronouncement. That he had the power to clear the skies or summon the rain or hurl down thunderbolts like a god. The story had passed into family lore: a little in-joke that had briefly lifted the mood at the funeral.

Then Jack had made the mistake of mentioning it on camera during *Bigwigs*, and the producers had run the clip over and over whenever they needed a contestant sob story. It didn't matter how many workplace challenges he led his team through; every time they played that stupid clip, it made him look like a dumb kid who believed his dad had superhuman powers.

"Terrible business," said Mr. Trench, after a pause. "But what makes the situation all the more tragic is the way this 'modern' world denies young chaps like yourself a clear-cut path from boyhood to manhood. That's why I founded the Lionheart Tigerwolf Self-Discovery Adventure Camp. Haven't looked back. Every month we go off camping in the Woodrose State Forest—sons, fathers, grandfathers—and hunt and fish and wrestle and just generally get in touch with our inner animal."

"Lionheart Tigerwolf?" said Jack. "That's a lot of inner animals to get in touch with, sir."

Mr. Trench opened his drawer and held up a sheet of paper. "Sign-up form's right here if you're interested."

"I'll think about it," said Jack.

"Very well," said Mr. Trench. "In the meantime, there's still the matter of this morning's incident in the student center. You seem to be claiming it was a misunderstanding. So answer me this, Sprigley: If you weren't gratifying yourself in front of your fellow pupils, what exactly *were* you doing?"

Jack sighed. "I was getting my phone out of my pocket. That's all. But something got stuck to my hand."

"Stuck to your hand?"

Jack realized he faced a dilemma. If he wanted to acquit himself of the public masturbation charge, he had to introduce Exhibit A: Pube Wig. "P-pardon?" he said, playing for time.

"What was it that got stuck to your hand?"

Jack took a long, deep breath. Things were already embarrassing enough without him pulling a homemade pubic thatch from his pocket. What sorts of embarrassing questions would Mr. Trench ask *then?* And as angry as Jack was with Philo for introducing the fateful merkin to his life, he didn't want to get the heir to Raisin World in trouble.

"I take it all back," said Jack. "It wasn't a misunderstanding. I actually was . . . doing what you said. Gratifying myself."

Mr. Trench gazed at him across the desk, his expression unreadable. Then he looked down, shuffled the papers on his desk, and said, "Oh well." He looked up and smiled. "Nothing to be ashamed of."

"P-pardon?" Jack said again, hardly believing what he'd heard.

Mr. Trench shrugged. "As I said, manhood is something you must take into your own hands. In the future, though, try not to take that advice quite so literally."

"So . . . does that mean I can go?"

"Permission granted. No disciplinary action required—though we *will* have to contact your mother, as a matter of formality."

"Really?"

"I'm afraid so. Until then, Sprigley, it's between you and me."

And the junior high's best and brightest, thought Jack. *And the staff-room cleaners, thanks to Mr. Trench.* And, if Hallie was right about the alcohol-buying thing, possibly all of the high school.

Not that it mattered who heard it now. Vivi had been right there in front of him.

Finally, Jack had proved to her that he really *was* too embarrassing to stay friends with.

Chapter Eleven

The bell rang. Jack hid behind the eighth-grade lockers, waiting for Philo to walk past.

"Psst!" he whispered.

Philo had opened up his locker and was dumping his books inside. "Jack, there you are! Everyone's talking about you."

"I wonder why *that* might be? Oh wait, it's *because of you and your stupid merkin!*" Jack thrust the pube wig at Philo.

Philo seemed reluctant to take the merkin back—which left Jack to hold it out between them like the worst Valentine offering in history.

"Jack, dude."

Jack turned around to see Reese and Darylyn standing behind him. He whisked the merkin out of sight, leaning casually against the lockers, hands behind his back, concealing the pube wig as best he could.

"So anyway," said Jack, raising his voice, "I can definitely help you with that homework problem, Philo."

Philo frowned and nodded insistently in the direction of the hidden merkin. "But what about the—"

"We'll talk later, okay?"

Jack thought he saw a hint of a pout on Philo's face as he turned and disappeared down the hallway. He felt a little bad. Maybe he'd hurt Philo's feelings. But Philo, with his ill-conceived act of crotch-crochet, had just about destroyed whatever was left of Jack's cred.

He nodded toward Reese and Darylyn, doing his best to play it cool. "H-hey guys. What's up? I haven't seen you two all morning."

Not exactly true, he thought.

Reese and Darylyn exchanged glances.

Jack grimaced. "When I say 'you two,' I don't mean there *is* a 'you two,' like that's a thing. I'm just saying, you're both here now. Together. Not 'together' together. Not that I'm saying you couldn't be. That'd be fine. If you were. I'm totally cool with all that stuff, obviously."

Darylyn shuffled closer to Reese and gave him a pointed nudge.

Reese scratched his jaw.

"So, dude. We . . . kind of heard about what happened."

Jack noticed Darylyn roll her eyes. Had she been expecting Reese to say something else? Had they actually come looking for him so they could fess up about their before-school rendezvous?

"It wasn't what it looked like," said Jack.

A bunch of tenth graders walked past. "Hey, it's Jack Spankley!" one of them shouted.

Jack did his best to ignore them. "I mean, lots of things aren't necessarily what they look like, right?" he said, looking at Reese and Darylyn. "You might see two people walking along and think, 'Is that person holding hands with that other person?' or you might see something else that's totally innocent and think, 'Hey, is that guy touching himself inappropriately in public?'—but actually, you might be completely wrong. And that's exactly what's happened here. Everyone's got it wrong."

He was about to gesture emphatically to drive home his point, but remembered he was still holding the merkin. He leaned against the lockers again to make sure it stayed hidden behind his back. "I mean, you don't really believe I'd . . . do *that* in front of everyone, do you?"

"I don't know, Jack. Yesterday you said you were doing it for the entire break," said Darylyn.

"Okay, fair point," said Jack. "But that was just . . . Look, it's under control. It's just a normal amount of completely nonpublic masturbation, the same as any other teenage male who has *definitely* hit puberty. I promise. Cross my heart."

Reese and Darylyn stared at him expectantly. Jack stood where he was, leaning against the lockers, not moving.

"Dude, are you crossing your fingers behind your back?"

"No!" said Jack.

Reese shrugged. "Well, whatever." He looked down at Darylyn, then back at Jack. "Look, this is kind of awkward. But there's something we've been meaning to tell you. Me and Darylyn, that is. Anyway . . . before the break, we kind of . . . well, we realized—"

"We realized we have feelings of affection for each other," said Darylyn. "Strong. Affection."

"Oh," said Jack. It felt like the time he'd pretended to be surprised when he opened the Xbox he'd seen in his mom's closet two weeks before Christmas. "Well . . . congratulations? And . . . thanks for telling me, I guess?"

"I told you he'd be weird about it," Reese muttered.

"I'm not!" said Jack. "Seriously. I've just had a pretty *intense* morning, okay? I think Mr. Trench tried to recruit me into some kind of wild-man cult. And possibly the army." He paused. "Wait, you thought I'd be weird about it?"

Reese looked uncomfortable. "It doesn't matter—"

"Jack?" came Vivi's voice down the hallway. Sampson

was with her, looking excited about the front-row seats he'd scored to yet another performance of the Jack Sprigley humiliation stage spectacular. "What the hell *was* that back there? Could you really not wait until Ditz-stagio had finished her speech? Seriously?"

"It wasn't what it looked like," said Jack. He had to admit it didn't sound any more convincing the second time around. Feeling under attack, he tried to back farther away, forgetting he was already fully pressed against the lockers.

"No?" snorted Sampson. "You're actually *not* an uncontrollable gherkin-jerker?"

Jack had to hold himself back from flipping Sampson the bird. For one thing, he still had the merkin in his hand. For another, Sampson would probably exact a terrible revenge next time they had PE.

"No," said Jack. "I'm not."

Vivi cocked her head to one side. "That's funny, because yesterday morning you decided to tell us all that you'd been masturbating for the *entire break*."

"Thank you," said Darylyn.

Jack groaned. "I've been through all this already."

"Sorry I missed it," said Vivi. "But we were busy filling in my application for Mayor for a Week."

"We?" said Jack.

"I had to get Oliver to nominate me."

"*I* hadn't been hauled away to see the vice principal," said Sampson, shrugging. "Plus I had the advantage of not having my hands full."

"Come on, dude," said Reese, frowning at Sampson. "Why are you even here?"

"It's okay, Reese," said Jack. "I can take a joke. I wouldn't want you thinking I'm being *weird* or anything."

Darylyn glanced at Reese, then Jack. "Well. This did not go the way I expected." She looked up at Sampson. "Also, I don't know who you are."

Just then Jack's phone buzzed in his pocket. He'd forgotten: Someone had been trying to call him. That was how the whole case-of-mistaken-masturbating had started.

With everyone busy talking to Sampson, Jack knelt down and threw the merkin into the bottom of his backpack, burying it beneath a pile of books.

With his hands and pockets finally free of pubic hairpieces, he grabbed his phone and checked his messages.

A missed call, a voice-mail message, and a bunch of texts, all from his mom.

I'm serious Jack! said the latest text. *Call me back NOW!!*

Mr. Trench had obviously called home already. Which meant the following conversation was going to be awkward.

Jack turned his back on Vivi and the others for a moment, took a deep breath, and pressed dial.

His mom's voice was high-pitched and breathless when she answered. "Jack?"

He sighed. "Hi, Mom."

There was a pause. "Well?"

"I . . . don't really know what to say."

"No, that's pretty much exactly how I felt!" said his mom.

"I guess they called you then."

"Yes, and they're going to send through an e-mail with more details."

Jack frowned. *More details?* "Wait, w-what sort of details did they give you?"

"Just the basics. When, where, how much."

"How *much*?"

"Then there's the big question, which is whether you want to do it again."

Do it again? Jack's brows drew together in confusion. He'd expected the conversation to be weird—but not *this* weird.

"It's your choice, obviously. I don't want you to do anything you're not comfortable with. But I just think, despite the way things ended up, you actually did have a lot of fun the first time, right?"

Jack couldn't believe what he was hearing. With the others still talking, he hunched over his phone and whispered, "Mom, this is kind of awkward. . . ."

"Okay. Let's talk it through properly tonight."

"Or . . . let's not?"

"Well, you'll have to decide sooner or later. But I understand. It's a lot to think about. But if you do decide to put yourself out there again, we'll have forms and things to fill out, so we'd want to get onto that ASAP."

"Forms?"

"Well, you'll need parental permission. Consent forms. They said they'll want to film you at school, at home, that kind of thing."

"*Film* me?" Was he being *monitored* now?

"Just a small crew. Then they want you to come onstage."

"Um—"

"I know, it could be a bit much with an audience and everything, but it's not a competition and you won't be on your own. There's going to be a whole bunch of you doing it, apparently."

"Wait wait wait wait wait," said Jack, putting a hand to his forehead. "The *school* wants to *film me* doing . . . *that*?"

Suddenly the others were looking his way. There was a pause on the other end of the phone. "Huh? Not the school, Jack."

"Well, who?"

"The *Bigwigs* people."

"*Bigwigs?*" said Jack.

"I told you. They want you to be on the show again. For this reunion thing they're doing. Didn't you listen to my message?"

Suddenly the whole conversation made a *lot* more sense—and had become roughly ten thousand times less disturbing.

"N-no," said Jack, breathing a sigh of relief. "No, sorry . . . I thought you were talking about something . . . totally different."

"What did you *think* I was—wait a minute, I've got another call coming through."

Jack realized it was probably Mr. Trench calling. "Don't answer it!" he blurted. He'd already suffered through one half of an awkward conversation—he wasn't sure he could repeat the experience with both sides fully briefed and up to date. "T-tell me more," he said, desperate to stop her answering the call.

He looked up at the others. "Tell me about this *Bigwigs* thing."

Chapter Twelve

Jack sat at the kitchen table with the laptop open in front of him. His mom stood behind him, one hand resting on his shoulder as they read and reread the e-mail from the *Bigwigs* producers.

We're kicking off an exciting new phase in the *Bigwigs* story, with the show about to enter its third year—the biggest yet—and its debut season in prime time. We feel there's no better way to celebrate where we've come from than to check in on our first-season contestants and find out what they're doing now. It's the perfect opportunity to show viewers how *Bigwigs* can change lives for the better.

In the coming weeks we'll send small crews to film our ex-contestants in their regular lives: at home, at school, and in their post-*Bigwigs* media careers. These segments will air during a special live reunion episode featuring all the contestants onstage together, to kick off the brand-new season of the show.

We'd be thrilled if Jack could join us for this one-of-a-kind episode of *Bigwigs*.

Jack scrolled through a whole section of appearance fee details and disclaimers and legal terms. There was a question-naire attached, where Jack was supposed to write down all the ways life had changed for him since he'd been on *Bigwigs*.

"They need an answer this week?" he asked.

"That's what it says," his mom said, looking over his shoulder. "It's weird: Weren't you just asking the other day if they'd been in touch? And now this. It's like it was *meant* to happen!"

Jack wasn't sure he liked how enthusiastic his mom was being. He tried to appeal to her sense of parental responsibility. "I'd have to miss a few days of school, though, to do the live show," he said.

Adele glanced sideways at him. "That might not be *such* a bad thing."

Despite Jack's best efforts, his mom had eventually heard Mr. Trench's message concerning "the incident" in the student center. Luckily, the message was so full of military jargon that Adele wasn't sure what Jack was supposed to be guilty of: inappropriate behavior at school or invading Pakistan.

Hallie, meanwhile, had clearly heard *all* about it. "You don't go anywhere *near* Nats from now on," she'd warned him, hauling him aside into the hallway just before dinner. "Don't even *think* about her. I'm *in* with those girls, and I don't need you *ruining it* for me."

Jack looked through the e-mail again. Maybe his mom was right. Doing the *Bigwigs* reunion show might be a way to take control of the story and save his reputation. A chance to steer the narrative toward "teenage boy makes triumphant return to semifame" and away from "teenage boy revealed to be public pants fondler."

Maybe it would even give him a second chance at being popular. Maybe everyone would be so starstruck by his return to TV, even just for a reunion episode, that they'd conveniently overlook how far he'd fallen behind them.

But could he really just slide back into the world of *Bigwigs* again?

Across the table, Marlene looked up from her phone, which she'd been fiddling with the whole time. "Can't say I like the idea of letting all those television cameras into the house."

"Come on, Mom, it's just *Bigwigs*. It's not *America's Most Wanted*." Adele squeezed Jack's shoulder. "It might be exciting to be back on TV again, don't you think? Catch up with all the other contestants? Reconnect? Maybe . . . take your mind off things?"

Would it, though? thought Jack. For some reason, he couldn't help thinking it might just make things worse.

As his mom poured herself another glass of wine, Jack brought up a browser window, swiveled the laptop slightly to the side, and typed *Bigwigs past contestants*.

Each new link he clicked on flashed up images of photo shoots and articles and magazine covers, some showing faces he only dimly remembered. YouTube uploads of Piers Blain's Byteface video blogs. Hope Chanders and the infamous anarchist symbol belly-button ring that had made her lose her recording contract with EMG/Platinum. Then there was Cassie Tau's Facebook addiction. And Mickey Santini's slightly too-choreographed wardrobe malfunction at the Teen Music Awards. And Amit Gondra's blossoming romance with sixteen-year-old Youth Olympics swimming hopeful Jessica Grouth. And there were others: contestants who'd become celebrity spokespeople and youth ambassadors and music video hosts and regular talk-show guests.

And then there was Jack. The only one, it seemed, who'd stayed where he was. Who'd stayed normal. Stayed the same.

As much as he wanted to yank himself free from the quicksand of loserdom he'd fallen into at school, this was one lifeline he didn't dare grasp. He was afraid that if he tried to use the *Bigwigs* reunion to rescue his reputation, he'd only sink further into a humiliation of national proportions. Because all the producers had to do was show one clip of Jack from when he'd been a contestant on the show, and the whole country would see that he looked and sounded the same as he had in sixth grade: fresh-faced and freckled, like a woodland creature in an old Disney cartoon.

The forums would melt down with hysterical disbelief. *"Did you see that Jack Sprigley kid? What a goddamn munchkin!" "I know! I heard he pretends to masturbate at school or something?"*

And it wouldn't just be the *Bigwigs* forums. The show was coming back bigger than ever. There'd be current affairs specials and newspaper columns and blogs and hashtags and comment threads all weighing in on his failure to pube it up.

The fact was, even among the former Bigwigs who'd had

brushes with the dark side of semifame, nothing anyone else had done was anywhere near as embarrassing as the things Jack's body had *failed* to do since sixth grade. So unless he was miraculously blessed with a pube-tacular growth spurt in the next week—when the *Bigwigs* people were expecting Jack's answer—he might be signing himself up for an online mauling as well as a schoolyard one.

The low-battery warning flashed up on the laptop screen. The short, stubby bar showing the currently available power was completely dwarfed by the long, forbidding tube representing a full charge.

Yeah, thought Jack. *That about sums it up.*

"I've pretty much decided," Jack said. "I'm not going to do it."

Reese nodded thoughtfully. They'd just turned the corner from Peppertree Drive and were a couple of blocks from school. "Good call. You did go kind of weird when those seventh graders unloaded about it the other day."

"That?" said Jack. "That was just me playing it cool."

"Uh-huh. Remind me to ask you more about this new definition of 'cool' sometime." Reese paused. "Still, respect. No point trying to compete with those other Bigwigs, dude. Not anymore."

Jack frowned. What did *that* mean? He turned to Darylyn. "What do you think, D?"

"I think we should swap places," said Darylyn.

Jack stopped. "You want to be on TV?"

Darylyn gave Jack a look. "I want to walk next to Reese."

"Oh," said Jack. He put on a "whoops!" face and took a step backward so that Darylyn could slide into his place. "Sorry."

Darylyn held out her hand toward Reese, who seemed paralyzed for a moment. Eventually Reese reached out his own hand, averting his eyes like he was trying to pass a note in class without being seen. It was only when his hand fumbled its way into contact with Darylyn's that Reese seemed to relax.

Great, thought Jack. *Now they're going to forget everything we were just talking about.* "Maybe I'll ask Vivi," he said, as the three of them got closer to the school gate. "Except then I'd have to deal with her new bestie, Sampson, chipping in his fifty cents. I mean, what a jerk, right?"

Reese shrugged. "He's okay."

"Are you serious? He called me a 'gherkin-jerker'!"

"Apparently you *are* a gherkin-jerker," said Darylyn.

Jack wanted to say that "gherkin-jerker" wasn't even the worst thing Sampson had called him. The others had no idea what had been said in the locker room, or on the soccer field. But what could he tell them? If he repeated Sampson's words, he'd be inviting suspicion that he was, in fact, a "baldy-balls."

Plus, it felt like tattling. He remembered Denny Trimble from *Bigwigs* being sent home for dissing Hope Chanders behind her back after Blue Team's mid-season loss in the "Host a First Grader's Birthday Party" challenge. It didn't seem like something a real man would do. A real man would settle the score one on one. But how could he possibly settle a score with someone who outmatched him as completely as Sampson did?

"He's still a jerk," Jack muttered.

"If you want my opinion," said Darylyn, "the smack-talking merely indicates a lack of social skills."

Reese nodded. "She's right. You should probably cut him some slack, dude. I don't think he's had much practice just hanging with peeps."

Jack couldn't believe what he was hearing. In what reality was Oliver Sampson—winner of puberty Powerball—some kind of tragic social outcast?

"Anyway," said Darylyn, "it looks like you don't have to worry." She pointed to the gate, where Vivi was waiting for them—without Sampson.

Speak of the devil, thought Jack, *and he shall . . . mysteriously be somewhere else.*

"Psst!" came a voice.

The three seventh-grade girls were lurking under a birch tree on the other side of the fence, next to where Jack was walking.

Jack hung back, glancing first at his friends, then back toward the seventh graders.

"What do you want?" he hissed.

They beckoned to him in unison. Jack wondered which one was ^kitty^cat, which one was {e-girrl}, and which one was Urchn. Then he realized he didn't know their real names either. Maybe those *were* their real names?

Reese and Darylyn were already through the gate and catching up with Vivi. Jack looked back at the seventh graders. On Monday they'd been bubbling over with excitement; now they looked deadly serious. They beckoned again—and before he knew it, Jack was at the fence.

"You were right," he told them. "They're bringing back the old contestants."

Jack thought he heard one of the girls whisper, "Bring back Jack."

"But I'm not doing it," he said, hurriedly. "I'm . . . almost certainly not doing it."

"Ignore the hater," said the first girl.

"What?" said Jack.

"Ignore . . . ," said the second girl.

". . . the hater," said the third.

"Wait," said Jack. "You mean on the forums?"

The three girls nodded solemnly in unison. "We're already on the case to uncover their true identity," the first one said.

"But we must seek help from higher powers," said the second girl.

"The *Bigwigs* forum administrators," the third girl intoned.

"Until then, we'll unleash a counterstrike of annoying emojis upon them until they withdraw," said the first girl.

The second girl fixed Jack with an earnest stare. "Meet us in the parking lot at the end of class. We'll have more to tell you. Until then, remember one thing. You *will* be a Bigwig again."

And then the three of them whispered together, "Ignore the hater. *Bring back Jack.*"

Chapter Thirteen

Jack found a carrel at the back of the library and slipped his laptop from his backpack.

An online hater. Just the thought of it made him feel jumpy. It was bad enough having Sampson lurking around, talking about Jack's fatal lack of pubes in front of everyone. Now there was some anonymous weirdo writing stuff about him on the Internet. Why now, all of a sudden?

The seventh graders had said they were looking into it. But first Jack wanted to know exactly what was being said about him.

He'd just loaded up the *Bigwigs* fan forum when he heard a familiar voice from the next carrel. "What do you mean, 'Search not allowed'?"

Jack rose from his seat and looked over the partition.

"Philo?"

Philo glanced up from his laptop, looking surprised. "Oh! Jack!" He folded down the laptop screen slightly. "Um . . . hi!"

"Having a problem?"

"No," said Philo, shrugging. "No problem. Just doing some . . . research."

This was worrying. "What sort of research?"

Philo bit his lip. "Nothing."

Jack sighed. "Not more merkins, Philo, *please*. Not after the trouble the last one got me into."

Philo closed the laptop and gathered it up off the desk. "No, not more merkels, Jack. But I've got a good feeling that things might be about to look up for you soon. In the pubes area, I mean! Sorry I can't stay and chat, though. I'll be in touch!"

Jack took a deep breath and sat back down. Whatever Philo was up to, it didn't sound good, but he didn't have time to worry about that now. He had a hater to track down.

Activity on the *Bigwigs* forum was building as the new season approached. The hardcore fans obviously knew about the past contestants coming back for some sort of reunion, but there were only guesses about when it might happen—at the start of the new season? Midway through? Just before the finals? There was also fevered speculation about who'd be returning and who wouldn't.

Jack was tempted to log on and tell the world that he was one ex-Bigwig who definitely *wouldn't* be. But then, in a random comment, Jack saw the word "Sprogless" scroll by.

He looked at the username attached to the post.

"ModLSkillz."

It didn't mean anything to him.

I heard that's what they call him at school. lmao srsly

Jack looked at ModLSkillz's profile. Whoever they were, they'd been a member of the forum for two years, but had only started posting the day before. Since then, ModLSkillz had written nearly a dozen posts, all in the same underhand, sneering tone, and all with the same target: Jack Sprigley.

Jack closed the laptop and stared blankly at the wall, thinking over what he'd seen.

The only person who'd ever called him "Sprogless" was Oliver Sampson. But surely there was no way Sampson would've made an account on the *Bigwigs* forum *two whole years ago*.

Jack met the girls as planned in the far corner of the staff parking lot. The bell had rung for third period, and the school grounds were slowly emptying again as Upland Junior

High's students and teachers marshaled themselves for the next stretch of the day.

Jack scraped his feet nervously against the asphalt as the seventh-grade girls approached. Each of them cradled a smoothie cup as though it were a crystal ball.

Jack lowered his voice. "So? Did you find anything out?"

"We have searched," said the first girl.

"We have found," said the second.

"We have your answer," said the third.

"Okay . . . ," said Jack.

The girls shared secretive glances and silently sucked on their smoothies. Finally the first girl lowered her cup and held Jack's gaze. "The username 'ModLSkillz' belongs to . . . someone at this school," she said.

Jack felt suddenly nervous.

"The person who has this username . . . is someone you know," said the second girl.

"No way," whispered Jack.

The third girl nodded. "The person with the username 'ModLSkillz' is . . . Oliver Sampson."

Jack nodded dumbly, processing the information. He wasn't completely shocked. In fact, now that he thought about it, he wasn't shocked at all. Sampson had basically gone from teasing Jack in the locker room to teasing him online. But it still didn't make sense that Sampson would have made an account on the *Bigwigs* forum two years ago.

"There's something else," said the first girl.

Jack looked up. "What do you mean?"

"Something else about Sampson," said the second girl.

As the other two girls sucked on their smoothies and traded conspiratorial glances, the third girl fixed Jack with her most serious and most beady stare.

"Something you definitely, *definitely* need to know."

The bell rang for lunch. Jack thought about grabbing some fries or a meat pie from the cafeteria, but then he remembered something about revenge being a dish best served cold, and got a ham and cheese sandwich instead.

He headed for the quadrangle and found the others already at the table. Sampson was there too. For once, Jack was actually pleased to see him.

Vivi and Darylyn looked on as Reese jammed his earbuds into a protesting Sampson's ears. At first Sampson pulled a "What the—?" face. But after a few moments of having his ears invaded by rocksteady Martian doo-wop or whatever other weirdness Reese had programmed for him, Sampson's face lit up with a "My life is changed!" glow.

Vivi looked up as Jack approached. "So did you decide already? Because I *really* don't want to be sitting next to you for the next two periods if you're going to be as spaced out as you were this morning." She turned to the others. "Mr. Jacobs had to call his name out three times in homeroom."

Jack nodded and looked at Sampson, who handed the earbuds back to Reese. "Actually, yeah. I have decided." He imagined Sampson at his keyboard, hammering out insults about Jack and sending his bitterness into the world for everyone to see. Because it all made sense now.

Jack shrugged. "It's a no-brainer, really."

Reese wound the earbuds back around his MP3 player. "I told you, dude. It's the right call."

"Agreed," said Vivi. She poked Jack in the arm. "Obviously *I* should be the center of attention right now that I'm officially in the running for Mayor—"

"I'm doing it," said Jack.

Reese nearly dropped his MP3 player. A flicker of shock passed across Vivi's face. Darylyn raised an eyebrow.

"I genuinely did not expect that," she said.

But there was only one reaction Jack cared about. He kept his eyes fixed on Sampson.

Oliver Sampson. Applicant for *Bigwigs* season two.

Application rejected.

It was almost too good to be true. But the seventh-grade girls had solid sources: They knew people who knew people who had older cousins who'd done internships in the *Bigwigs* production office. Somehow, they'd traced the "ModLSkillz" tag to an application from Oliver Sampson. And for whatever reason, Sampson had been rejected. Jack didn't care why. All he knew was that he had the upper hand for once.

Sampson went quiet for a moment. "You're going to be on *Bigwigs* again?" he said, finally.

"It's a reunion special," said Jack. "Me and the other past contestants. It's weird, you know—in some ways, you never really *stop* being a Bigwig. It probably seems weird to someone who's never actually been a Bigwig themselves—"

"Well, it's pretty brave of you," Sampson butted in.

Everyone turned to look at him.

"Brave?" said Jack, frowning. "Why?"

"I mean, it's not like you've actually *changed* at all, Sprigley. Everyone's going to think there's something *wrong* with you." With that, Sampson forced his way past Jack and took the closest exit from the quadrangle—nearly knocking over a couple of tenth graders on the way.

"We'll see," Jack called after him, trying to sound more confident than he felt. He'd already texted his mom. She was probably e-mailing the producers as he spoke. It was basically a done deal.

He turned to the others and shrugged. "I think people might be surprised. They might not even recognize me."

Vivi gave Jack a look. "What do you mean 'might'?"

Part Two

Bigwigging

Chapter Fourteen

Jack's bed sat at an awkward angle in the middle of the bungalow. Boxes full of books and magazines and comics were stacked against the wall near the doorway to the tiny bathroom.

"So where do you think the bed should go?" Jack asked Philo.

Philo appeared to be deep in thought. "On the floor," he concluded.

Jack sighed and threw himself onto the bed. "It doesn't matter, I'll decide later. At least all the big stuff's shifted in now. Thanks a lot for helping me, Philo."

Philo sat at the foot the bed. He was supposed to be

manning the Raisin World stand at the Upland Tourist Information Center, but apparently he'd persuaded his parents to let him have a rare Saturday off. "It's no bother, Jack. I could do this all day!"

Lucky, thought Jack. They'd been moving furniture since eight in the morning.

First, they'd moved all of his gran's things out of the bungalow and piled them up in the back room of the house. There were still a few things to move out of Jack's room—garbage bags full of his clothes, his schoolbag, and a few miscellaneous oddities from under his bed—before they could start moving Marlene's things in.

They'd already shifted so many boxes and moved so many pieces of furniture that Jack's arms and legs were throbbing in places he doubted he'd even grown muscles yet. Philo, though, showed no sign of flagging. He seemed able to lift heavy objects with the power of cheerfulness alone. He hadn't even complained when Jack had dropped a chest of drawers on his toe. (Jack suspected that he hadn't actually noticed.)

"It's a bummer that Vivi and the others couldn't help. We could've had everyone pitching in together!"

"Yeah . . . ," said Jack. He hadn't actually told them about his plan to move into the bungalow. "They're being kind of immature about it, to be honest. They don't really get the whole 'keeping up with the other Bigwigs' thing."

"Oh, so *all* the other Bigwigs are moving into their own apartments?"

"Not all of them," said Jack. "Just Piers Blain."

"But not you?"

"Yes, me! What do you think we're doing right now?"

"But this isn't an apartment. It's a bungalow."

"Bachelor pad."

"Right. So where are the other Bigwigs moving to?"

"Nowhere! But they've got other stuff going on. Amit Gondra's got a totally hot girlfriend who's *older* than him. Girlfriends, boyfriends, Internet addictions, belly-button piercings . . . they've all changed in, like, really obvious ways."

Philo gave him a solemn look. "Jack, I really don't think you should get your belly button pierced."

"I was joking, Philo. I'm *clearly* not going to get my belly button pierced. That would look ridiculous." (He decided he'd probably just get a tattoo.) "Come on," he said, "we'd better finish moving Gran's stuff."

Philo followed Jack out of the bungalow and into the midday heat. A badly timed taste of summer was blowing through Upland. Jack wished it had come on a day when he *wasn't* shifting heavy furniture around. He opened the sliding door into the back room of the house, where they were met by the sight of Hallie, fresh from the shower, surveying the pile of Marlene's belongings with a pained look on her face.

"What's all this crap still doing here? No offense, Gran."

Marlene, who'd found a corner of the back room where she could escape the mess, glanced up from her phone. "Hmm?"

"I said, Jack *still* hasn't moved your stuff."

Marlene rolled her eyes. "Tell me about it, dear."

"We've just got a few more things to move out of my room," said Jack.

"I can't believe this is even happening," said Hallie. She called out to Adele, who was busy unloading some supermarket shopping in the kitchen. "I said, *I can't believe this is even happening!*" She turned back to Jack. "But then, why should I be surprised? You always get special treatment. I just didn't think she'd *actually* let you kick Gran out of her bungalow."

"I didn't kick her out. It was an agreement. Wasn't it, Gran?"

"Y-yes," said Marlene. "Something like that."

In fact, Marlene had been totally against the idea at first. "But Jack, I'd lose all my privacy!" she'd complained. Which had immediately got Jack thinking about how strange she'd been acting when he'd dropped off her prescription, and how she'd been furtively checking her phone all week. He had no idea why she was being so secretive. All that had mattered to Jack was that he had a bargaining position. He'd felt his *Bigwigs* mojo coming back to him.

"I see . . . ," he'd said, narrowing his eyes and rubbing his chin. "Interesting."

"What is, dear?"

"Your reason for not wanting to swap rooms. Privacy. *Very* interesting." He'd paused, keeping her in suspense. "It *almost* suggests there's something you're doing you don't want anyone to know about. . . ."

That was all it had taken. Suddenly the bungalow was Jack's. Frankly, even Jack was surprised at how easy it had been. She couldn't have minded the switch *too* much.

Hallie shook her head. "So unfair."

"It's just for this *Bigwigs* thing," said Jack.

"I know," said Hallie, looking at him darkly. "*Everything's* about *Bigwigs*. You don't need to remind me."

Adele had finished unloading the groceries. "What's all the shouting about? Oh! You're still here, Philo."

"Hello again, Mrs. Sprigley," said Philo.

Adele glanced meaningfully at Jack and Hallie. "Maybe we could avoid having an argument while there's a Dawson in the house?"

"There wouldn't *be* a Dawson in the house if you hadn't let Jack move into Gran's bungalow! Now the whole house is a disaster zone, and I've got people coming over in, like, ten minutes!"

"What? Who's coming over?" said Jack.

"She's going to the pool with Natsumi Distagio," said his mom. "Aren't you, Hallie?"

Hallie groaned. "Great. It's not enough that Jack gets *everything* he wants. Now he's going to stand around ogling my friends."

"I'm not a pervert," said Jack.

"Oh, so you'll actually keep your grubby little hands out of your pockets this time?"

"It wasn't what it looked like," Jack muttered.

The doorbell rang.

Jack turned to Philo. Meeting Nats in the flesh was a chance for Jack to show everyone that he wasn't a pervert or a weirdo, despite certain evidence to the contrary. But there was no way he could risk the Philo factor. The potential for embarrassment was too great. "Hey, Philo, I was thinking maybe you could start clearing the rest of the stuff out of my room?"

"Sure thing, Jack!"

Philo zipped off down the hallway.

"You know what?" Hallie grabbed her tote bag and beach towel from the kitchen bench. "I don't want Jack humiliating me. I'm not even going to let them insi—"

"It's open!" shouted Adele.

Jack heard the sound of heels on the slate tiles in the foyer.

"Hello? Hals?" came a voice.

And there she was, standing in the space between the foyer and the kitchen. High-heeled sandals, loose white dress over her bikini, hair impossibly golden.

Natsumi Distagio.

Adele welcomed her in.

"It's Natsumi, isn't it? I'm Adele, Hallie's mom." She paused. "And since Hallie's obviously not going to make the introductions, that's my mother, Marlene . . . and this is Jack. Jack Sprigley. Obviously," she added.

Nats smiled at Adele and Marlene. Then she turned to Jack, and a look of recognition passed across her face. She frowned and tilted her head to one side. "I'm sure I've seen you somewhere recently. You look *really* familiar. . . ."

Jack realized she was probably thinking of the spectacle he'd made of himself at the Mayor for a Week information session. He had to act fast.

"Maybe you just recognize me from TV?" he said nervously.

"Oh, were you in one of those Raisin World ads?"

Jack shook his head. "No, not Raisin World."

"Avocado World?"

"Jack was on national TV," said Adele. "He was on *Bigwigs*. You know, that reality show? And he's about to go on it again, aren't you, Jack?"

Jack tried to ignore Hallie's sharp intake of breath. Nats looked at him in awe. "National TV? Really?"

He shrugged nonchalantly.

Nats nudged Hallie. "Hals, you didn't tell me your brother was a TV star!" Her eyes grew wide as she said "TV star."

"That's because he's not. It was just a dumb reality show for kids."

"I *really* want to be on TV one day," said Nats.

"Really?" said Jack. "Because if there's anything you want to know—"

"I want to know *everything*!" said Nats.

Jack realized what a momentous occasion this was. His first meeting with Natsumi Distagio—and right away it seemed they had so much in common. He'd been on TV, she *wanted* to be on TV. . . .

"What's it like?" Nats asked.

Jack stared back at her. "It's like . . . being in a dream."

He realized he wasn't just describing what it was like being on TV—it was also how he felt being appraised by those soft, brown eyes. It didn't seem possible this could be happening to him.

"Maybe I could go on one of those supermodel shows," said Nats.

"Yeah, definitely," said Jack. "I mean, you've got the body for it."

Adele cleared her throat nervously. Marlene glanced up from her phone. Hallie shot him a look of icy censure.

"*A* body," said Jack. "You've got a *complete* body. N-not that people with less than the usual number of body parts can't be models. I think you'd probably win one of those supermodel shows even with a bunch of limbs missing."

"Oh God," said Hallie.

"*Limbs* missing?" said Nats.

Hallie stepped between Nats and Jack, trying to usher Nats out of the house.

"*This* is why I wanted to just meet you guys at the pool. I *told* you it was a mistake to come here."

"But I wanted to!" Nats turned to Adele. "My parents say that family is the most important thing in the world, and I truly believe that."

Hallie glanced warily at Nats. "Well, just don't hold it against me?"

"Hals, what are you talking about? Your brother was on *TV!* That's a major plus!"

Hallie rolled her eyes. "Maybe we should get going?"

Nats seemed to shake herself free of the spell that Jack's fame had cast over her. She rattled her car keys in her hand. "Yeah, I guess we should make a move. Yaz and Stace are waiting."

Just then, Philo wandered into the back room from the hallway, wearing a querying look on his face.

"Jack, I tripped over your schoolbag and found this."

Jack looked at what Philo was holding. Not that he was really *holding* it so much as *waving it in the air*.

Marlene and Adele squinted, trying to work out what exactly they were looking at. Nats frowned. Hallie looked faint.

Philo held the merkin up and looked at it, like a ventriloquist exchanging dialogue with his puppet. "I wasn't sure if you wanted it in with your jocks and socks or—"

Jack thought fast. He needed to divert attention from the question of *why* he'd been keeping a bundle of pubes in his room, without giving anything *else* away—like, for instance, the fact that they were the only pubes he had at all. "How . . ." He made a show of seeming confused, looking down at his shorts and then at the merkin, as if the latter were a bundle of his own actual pubes that had somehow escaped and made a run for it. He looked up at Nats and the others with a "What the—?" expression. "H-how did they . . . how did my . . . how did *those* get over *there?*"

"Oh God," said Hallie. "*Oh God.*"

Just then, Adele's cell phone buzzed. Jack took the opportunity to shove Philo back down the hallway. Hallie was already dragging Nats out of the house, apparently trying to get as much distance from Jack as possible. Nats waved a quick good-bye over her shoulder.

Meanwhile, Adele listened to the voice at the other end of the phone. She nodded and made "mmm-hmm" noises, then glanced up at Jack and mouthed *"Bigwigs."* She nodded some more, then said, "Great. Tomorrow morning. We'll see you then!"

Tomorrow morning? thought Jack. The bungalow was only halfway to becoming a proper bachelor pad. He had a long way to go to catch up to the other Bigwigs. But on the plus side, he could roll into school on Monday and tell Sampson he'd already spent a whole day in front of the *Bigwigs* cameras.

As for catching up to the other Bigwigs, maybe it wasn't going to be as hard as he thought. Amit Gondra may have had Jessica Grouth, but Jack, completely unexpectedly, had just managed to lay down some pretty impressive ground-work with *Natsumi* freaking *Distagio.*

Bring back Jack, he thought. *Bring back Jack.*

Chapter Fifteen

s soon as Jack woke the next morning he hooked his thumb under the elastic on his pajama bottoms, closed one eye, and peered down into the nether-world under his sheets.

Still no change.

He'd hoped that spending his first night in his brand-new bachelor pad might have supercharged his gonads into action. That was the golden scenario: hitting his growth spurt just in time for the *Bigwigs* cameras to capture his sudden transformation into proper fourteen-year-old man-liness.

But it looked as though he'd have to fake it after all, and

hope that *something* started to happen gonad-wise in the next few weeks, before the live onstage reunion.

He'd spent the night before making the bungalow look as spartan and stylish and bachelor pad-ish as possible. Even then, he was worried it didn't properly signal maturity and sophistication, so he'd snuck out to the twenty-four-hour supermarket on his bike and bought a dozen canisters of shaving cream to put on display in the bungalow's bathroom.

"There's no discount for buying twelve," the cashier had told him.

"Tell me about it," said Jack. "Also, can I have a bag?"

Fake it until you make it. That was something Hope Chanders used to say back on *Bigwigs*, whenever Blue Team fell short in one of their assignments. She'd had no problem looking straight at the camera during a location piece and spinning some huge lie about how she'd single-handedly produced her elementary school's newsletter, or that she'd been captain *and coach* of her Pee Wee hockey team, just so she got the project manager gig week after week.

That was the secret, Jack realized. Sampson seemed to think everyone would immediately spot that Jack hadn't changed. But what did Sampson know? He wasn't the one who'd actually been on the show before. He didn't know how TV worked. He didn't know that being on TV meant you could change the way people saw you—as long as you gave the camera the right information.

Jack hadn't known that the first time around. But he knew it now.

The *Bigwigs* crew arrived at nine thirty, pulling up in a rented minibus. There were three of them: a woman in her twenties (Jack guessed) with her hair in a tight ponytail, wearing a skirt, tights, Converse shoes, and a baggy striped cardigan; and two guys in black jeans and black muscle shirts. Jack peered out from behind the front curtain as they unloaded their cameras and lights and sound equipment. One of the guys—the one who was currently in the process of assembling a boom mike, and whose T-shirt was stenciled with heavy metal album artwork—had the sort of beard Jack had only ever seen worn by Jesus and people who hung out with Jesus.

Marlene had made herself scarce, heading off early to one of her retirees' club lunches. Hallie was either out with Nats and the Shieling twins, or had locked herself in her room—Jack wasn't sure.

Jack watched as his mom went out to meet the crew. He wished he'd gone out instead. He realized he'd missed a prime opportunity to present himself as the man of the house. Now he needed to make a proper entrance when the crew stepped through the front door. Jack sped away to the back of the house, out through the glass door. He rushed into the bungalow, made straight for the bathroom, pawed half the canisters of shaving cream into the crook of his arm, and raced back into the house again.

Adele was showing the crew into the kitchen just as Jack made his breathless return to the house.

"I'll tell you what, I've been going through *these* like nobody's business," he loudly declared, tipping the canisters into the kitchen bin. "Shaving cream," he added, in case it hadn't been obvious. He looked around at the crew and suddenly noticed how much more bristly and velvety and basically *frightening* the sound guy's beard was up close. He wondered how much shaving cream it would take to get through *that*.

The woman in the striped cardigan and Converse stood up and held out her hand.

"Hi, Jack, I'm Delilah. Delilah Trick." She gestured to her crew. "This is Todd, and over there with the camera is Brett."

Jack tore his eyes away from Todd's beard and shook Delilah's hand firmly. He gave her a brisk, manly nod. "Delilah. Don't remember the name. New to *Bigwigs*?"

"I am! This is my first year on the show."

"Yeah, I'm an old hand. Been around the *Bigwigs* block a few times. Stick with me, kiddo: You'll be all right."

There was an awkward silence. Todd and Brett exchanged glances.

Delilah looked slightly baffled. "Well . . . thanks. Thanks, Jack, I'll do that. You know, it's so great to be bringing you back to *Bigwigs*. I was just saying, we were watching some of your clips on the flight here, getting up to speed. I was back-packing through South America when your season of *Bigwigs* was on so I missed it the first time around. You were brilliant! And you've hardly changed at all! This is going to be great!"

Great? thought Jack. His very first face-to-face contact with anyone from *Bigwigs* and they'd spotted within *seconds* that he was still the same Jack Sprigley from two years ago.

Adele set about making coffee for Delilah and her two-man crew. Delilah checked her phone for messages. "It'd be great if I could get onto your Wi-Fi, Adele?"

"There's Wi-Fi out in the pad," said Jack nonchalantly. "Five bars."

Delilah seemed to remember something. "Right!" she said. "Your mom was saying you have your own bungalow out back. That's so cool! Maybe that's where we should do the first piece-to-camera?"

Excellent, thought Jack. He needed to make a good first impression.

This part, at least, was going according to plan.

Jack had left the bathroom door open wide enough that the remaining shaving cream canisters could be seen sitting in the bathroom cabinet. He checked out where Brett the cameraman was setting up, hoping the canisters would be in shot.

"So, Jack, we never actually got your questionnaire back," said Delilah, glancing at her phone. "About how things have changed since *Bigwigs*."

"Yeah, sorry about that," said Jack. "It's just . . . there were too many changes for one questionnaire, really. I mean, obviously there's this. . . ." He gestured around the bungalow.

Delilah looked around, swiftly scrutinizing every corner like a detective gathering evidence. She turned back to Jack. "You know, Piers Blain is about to move into his own place too."

"Is he?" Jack rolled his eyes. "About time! Seriously, the first thing I did after *Bigwigs* was spend my prize money on fixing this place up—" (*Totally true,* he thought to himself.) "—and then I moved straight in." (*Totally not true,* he thought to himself.) "Yeah, I've been doing the bachelor pad thing for *quite a while* now." He paused. "Wait, you're filming this?"

Brett nodded.

Jack didn't remember the camera lens seeming so intimidating, like it was peering into his soul. He must have gotten used to it quickly, the first time. He'd been able to be himself. That wasn't an option this time.

"So . . . this bachelor pad business. Tell us more about that."

They'd been filming in stops and starts for half an hour. Delilah had started off chirpy and interested, but Jack had the feeling she was getting bored.

"Um . . ." He looked around the room, trying to think of something interesting to say.

"I guess I'm thinking more of the 'bachelor' part," said Delilah. "I'm sure everyone will want to know: Is Jack Sprigley looking for love? Or is there already someone on the scene?"

Jack thought of Amit Gondra and Jessica Grouth. He thought of his unexpected encounter the day before. "Well, it's early days. . . ."

Delilah looked searchingly at him and smiled. "But?"

Jack started to sweat. "But . . . yeah? There . . . might be someone?"

"Uh-huh," said Delilah, conspiratorially, her interest suddenly sparked. "And does this mystery girl or boy have a name?"

"Her name," said Jack. "You want to know her name. Well, that's kind of an interesting story . . . because . . . actually, I know it seems weird, but she doesn't technically *have* a name."

Todd and Brett turned to each other. Delilah raised her eyebrows. "She doesn't have a name?"

Jack mentally face-palmed himself. "No, I mean, obviously she *does* have a name. That would be . . . insane, if she didn't. So the name, that she has, is . . . well, it's Nats." He cleared his throat self-consciously. "Natsumi."

"Natsumi?" Delilah tapped something into her phone. "I have to say, Jack, that's quite a long way from not having a name! It's actually a very *interesting* name."

"Yep," said Jack, nodding in agreement. "It *is* an interesting name." *What's* particularly *interesting, he thought, is how I just said it out loud. On camera. For the whole country to eventually hear.* He leaned toward Delilah and whispered, "Off the record, you're not going to use *all* the stuff we're filming here, right?"

Delilah shrugged. "Somehow or other we probably will. You know how this works. Obviously we'll do some cutting—"

"Maybe you could just cut all of it!" Jack suggested with a laugh. He noticed the camera was still rolling.

"Why?" said Delilah, frowning. "It's going great! We're getting to know you! Maybe Natsumi would like to be on camera at some stage too?"

Jack was sure she would. But being wrongfully outed as a fourteen-year-old's pretend girlfriend probably wasn't what she had in mind.

"The bachelor pad thing is really cool, by the way. It's like you're a feudal lord in your castle."

Jack shrugged. "Well, it's a big responsibility, being man of the house. And a burden, I guess, if I'm being honest. I kind of need my man-space. So I can do my . . . man-things."

"But you'd rather you didn't have to?"

"Huh?"

"What I mean is, do you feel like you've had to grow up too fast? Because of your dad not being around? You said it felt like a burden."

Jack swallowed. He hadn't expected Delilah to ask about his dad. He hoped it wasn't going to be like *Bigwigs* season one, with the whole sob-story angle. He tried to play it cool. "Yeah, I guess that's true. I guess I *have* grown up fast. That'll be . . . pretty obvious to everyone watching this, I hope. But a burden?" He tried to look reflective. "Only in the sense of having a *lot* more to carry downstairs all of a sudden, if you know what I mean."

Delilah glanced around the room, as if searching for a trapdoor somewhere. "There's a downstairs?"

"You know what? Forget I said that. The point is, I'm okay with it. Stepping up. Being the man of the house. It's all good."

An image of his dad's bathrobe and slippers flashed into Jack's head. He froze. His throat went tight. No, it wasn't all good at all. The times when he did stop to think about it, he couldn't decide what was worse: his dad being gone, and how much that hurt, or the fact that sometimes he let himself forget. Either way, the camera was still on him. He had to keep faking it.

"So there hasn't been anyone else? Your mom hasn't . . ."

Delilah must have noticed Jack trying to look away from the camera, trying to wriggle out from under the glassy stare of the lens.

"Sorry," she said. "I didn't mean to . . ." She glanced at Todd and Brett. "I think we can wrap up there for now."

Jack was relieved to see the red light on the camera switch to black. He asked Delilah if she had everything she needed.

Delilah bunched her mouth up, looking apologetic. "I'd kind of like to get some more footage of you around the house, with your family, if that's okay? I'm thinking, for dinner: Do you usually have a sit-down meal or—"

"Probably a barbecue," said Jack, without thinking.

"A barbecue?"

"Yeah, it's a bit of a weekend tradition. Me, cooking sausages on the barbie. It turns out I'm *quite* the tong-master."

Delilah turned to her crew. "We could film a barbecue. Yeah, that could actually work out well. Nice visual."

"Great," said Jack through a tight smile. "That's . . . really great that we're doing that." He nodded and clapped his hands together. "Well. I guess we'll be needing sausages."

Chapter Sixteen

~~~~~~

Jack had tried to suggest that a visit to the supermarket to get sausages possibly wasn't exactly what *Bigwigs* fans would be craving when they tuned in to the big reunion special, but Delilah said they needed all the footage they could get. "It's all part of the story," she'd told him.

He had to pretend to pay for the sausages four times for the camera. The first time, the cashier had giggled nervously and ruined the shot; the second time, Jack fumbled his change and dropped it all over the floor; and the third time, old Davo had wandered past in his red, white, and blue silk tracksuit, stuck his head into the shot, and shouted, "What are ya doin', buyin' sausages, are ya?"

With the sausages finally secured, Delilah had asked Jack if they could get some footage of him walking down the main street. Luckily, because it was Sunday, the main street was relatively free of onlookers. Those who did crowd around were expertly kept at bay by Delilah, without them actually noticing they were being kept at bay. They gazed at Jack with mild awe, as though the fact that he had a camera pointed at him meant that he couldn't possibly be an ordinary mortal.

Embarrassing as it was, Jack also kind of enjoyed the feeling it brought back: the feeling of being big. It was exactly why he'd signed on to do the reunion special. To show everyone he was bigger than—

"Sampson!" said Jack, stopping dead in his tracks.

Delilah's ears seemed to prick. Brett looked up from his viewfinder. Whispers spread through the small crowd.

Sampson had stepped out of the newsstand two doors down and was staring over at Jack and the crew. Jack noted with a satisfied smirk that he looked slightly daunted by the sight of the camera and the boom mike.

Delilah seemed to be assessing the situation. She nodded at Brett, who hoisted his camera up again and focused on the viewfinder.

"Do you two know each other?" asked Delilah.

Jack realized he needed to get the upper hand quickly.

He took a deep breath, remembering what the seventh-grade girls had told him about Sampson trying to get onto *Bigwigs* the year after Jack—and failing.

"We're just starting to know each other!" he said. "Starting to get to know *a-l-l* kinds of things about each other."

"I . . . know Jack from school," Sampson mumbled. "Junior high . . . and elementary school."

Jack found it hard to remember that Sampson had even *been* to elementary school, he'd seemed fully grown for so long.

"Oh!" said Delilah. "So you'd probably remember Jack being on *Bigwigs*?"

Sampson shook his head. "Never watched it."

Lies, thought Jack. "Oh, you *really* missed out," he said.

"I've seen some of the old contestants on TV, though," said Sampson, sounding more confident all of a sudden. He narrowed his eyes at Jack cunningly. "You know, Piers Blain on YouTube and stuff. And Hope Chanders is a VJ on *Charturday Morning*, right? Wow, they've all gone on to bigger and better things, haven't they? Well, *most* of them."

Delilah tapped something into her phone. "What was your name again?"

"Sampson. Oliver Sampson."

Jack realized that Sampson had probably dreamed of saying his name in front of the *Bigwigs* cameras. He wondered if this was how he'd always pictured it.

"So, Oliver: Were you surprised when Jack didn't show up on our screens again after *Bigwigs*?"

Sampson snorted. "No. I wasn't surprised at all."

Jack glanced back and forth down the street. He needed a Davo to wander in and ruin the take. He turned to Brett behind the camera. "H-how's the battery going there, chief? We've done *so* much filming already it's bound to be running low—"

"We're good," said Brett.

"We might stop there anyway," said Delilah. "But Oliver, can I get some details from you? You're under sixteen, right?"

Come on, thought Jack. *He doesn't look* that *old.* Then he thought for a moment longer and realized that, yes, Sampson actually *did* look that old.

Sampson nodded.

"Okay," said Delilah. "In that case, I'll need to forward a release form to a parent or guardian."

Delilah quizzed Sampson to get his address. Jack felt a stab of fear, mixed with a pang of something else. Maybe . . . jealousy?

He hadn't counted on Sampson barging into his *Bigwigs* shoot like this. Jack hoped he hadn't just given Sampson exactly what he wanted.

Jack's mom had some bad news when Jack and the others returned home from the sausage-buying mission.

"How can we not own a barbecue?" said Jack.

Adele held out her hands.

"I don't know how to answer that! If you'd *told* me that was what you were doing, instead of being Mr. 'I'm in Charge,' I could have warned you!" She looked in the supermarket bag sitting on the kitchen bench. "And why did you buy *eleven pounds* of sausages?"

"It's okay, *Bigwigs* paid for it."

"It's not about who paid for it. We're never going to get through that many sausages! I can barely convince Hallie to eat *anything* these days."

"Delilah said we might need extra, in case they don't get the footage they need. They're basically stunt sausages."

Adele sighed. "Well, you'll have to just cook them on the stove inside."

"Not exactly 'man conquers nature,' is it?" said Jack.

Adele's face softened. She looked at Jack as though she wanted to say something, but then changed her mind.

"I think there's an old camping stove in the shed," she said, finally.

Brett and Todd waited around while Delilah made some phone calls from the van out front. Jack rummaged in the kitchen cupboards for a frying pan large enough to cook the apparently excessive number of sausages he'd bought, but not so large that it would crush the legs of the flimsy kerosene burner beneath it. Meanwhile, the manliest apron he'd been able to find had orange and white diagonal stripes across it and reached all the way down to his shins.

He did not have a good feeling about "the sausage segment."

He set the camping stove up on a trestle table in the backyard and did his best to balance the frying pan on it. By this time Delilah had returned. She murmured instructions to Brett as he tried to get a few different angles on Jack's struggles with his improvised barbecue.

Eventually Jack gave up. He looked up at Delilah, hoping the pleading look in his eyes didn't come across as being too pathetic. "Um, this really isn't working."

Delilah shared a look with Brett, then nodded. "Okay, let's mercy-kill this one." She gave Jack a shrug and a smile. "It's okay, we've got plenty of time. We'll get some great footage tomorrow at school, I'm sure."

Jack nearly dropped his tongs. "School?"

"Tomorrow's Monday, right?"

"Yeah, but . . ." Jack swallowed hard. His stock had fallen drastically low at school. What if someone shouted out "Jack Spankley" while the camera was rolling? How would he explain *that* away? Then again, maybe all the other students would fall silent as soon as they saw the cameras and sound equipment, the way the onlookers on the main street had done. Maybe the glare of the TV spotlight would eclipse all of his past embarrassments.

But there was still the Natsumi Distagio situation. Somehow he had to keep her away from Delilah and the whole *Bigwigs* thing—at least until he'd had a chance to warn her about the massive lie he'd blurted out on camera. Warn her—or maybe convince her to go along with it?

Better still, make her his *actual* girlfriend.

"Are you okay, Jack?"

Jack snapped back to reality. Delilah was staring at him.

"Yeah. Sure. Just . . . well, I don't know if they actually *allow* filming at the school. There's forms and things, probably."

"It's all been cleared," said Delilah. "Trust us! We're professionals. We've got all the right permits. We know what we're doing."

I'm glad someone does, thought Jack. He was starting to wonder if he'd made a massive mistake agreeing to do the reunion show.

"That Sampson guy seems interesting," said Delilah, casually, as she leaned over to look into the camera viewfinder, inspecting the day's footage. She looked up at Jack.

"It'd be good to include him in the filming tomorrow some-how. What do you think?"

I think I've definitely made a massive mistake, Jack said to himself.

Chapter Seventeen

ack waited at the school gate, checking his watch. He felt like a bit of a dork, turning up to school almost a whole hour before the bell. He might as well have brought an apple for Mr. Jacobs.

Finally Delilah and her crew pulled up in their rented minivan. Delilah was in the front passenger seat, talking on the phone. She waved at Jack when she noticed him waiting by the gate, ended her call, and climbed out of the van while Brett and Todd unloaded their gear.

"Sorry about the early start," she said. "We want to get as much footage as possible before you head into class." She took a sip from the coffee she'd obviously bought on the way from her motel, then brought up some notes on her phone. "So you said you'd be meeting some of your friends first, right?"

Jack nodded, but he worried he was being slightly optimistic. He hadn't seen Vivi, Reese, or Darylyn all weekend. Not that that was anything new: He'd gone all of winter break without seeing them. But things had gotten even weirder since Jack had told everyone he was going back on *Bigwigs*.

"Do we have those releases ready?" Delilah called to Brett. He slid a blue folder halfway out of his camera bag, which seemed to satisfy her. "Our agreement with your principal covers any filming inside the school grounds, but your friends will have to get these signed by their parents if they're going to appear with you on camera."

Jack was still uneasy about being filmed at school. There were too many variables beyond his control. Variables like the shouting out of not-very-subtle references to his incident in the student center by passing tenth graders. Variables like Oliver Sampson. Variables like Natsumi Distagio. He didn't like having to think about variables. Even very sexy ones.

"Well, most of the really exciting stuff I do happens outside of school hours," he said. *Like purchasing—and failing to cook—a large quantity of sausages,* he thought to himself.

"We need to get coverage on every part of your life," said Delilah. "You know how it is—we have to find the story. Take these two, for instance."

Jack looked across the road to where Delilah was pointing.

"I can tell right away there's something going on between them," said Delilah. "A spark. An energy. But there's something else. They're not totally at ease with each other. Like they've been forced to hide something, or—"

"Hey, Reese," said Jack. "Hey, Darylyn."

Reese and Darylyn crossed the road and warily approached Jack and the *Bigwigs* crew. Reese took one look at Todd's heavy metal T-shirt and retreated into his earbuds, starstruck.

No sooner had Reese and Darylyn arrived than Jack saw the school bus pull up farther down the street.

The first two students to get out were Vivi Dink-Dawson and Oliver Sampson.

Sampson fist-bumped Reese and Darylyn. "Hey, it's Research and Development!"

Jack looked at Sampson blankly.

"R&D?" said Sampson. "Reese and Darylyn?"

"You're such a dork, Oliver," said Vivi.

Jack couldn't believe what he was hearing. Nobody was allowed to be a jock *and* a dork.

"This is Vivi," Jack said, introducing her to Delilah. "We've been friends since the start of junior high." He inserted himself between Sampson and Vivi. "All four of us: me, Vivi, Reese, Darylyn. 'The gang.'"

"Hi, folks," Delilah said. Then she glanced at Sampson. "We meet again!"

Jack barreled on before Sampson had a chance to reply. "The cool thing about Vivi is that she's applying to be Upland's Mayor for a Week this year. Pretty amazing. Almost like a *Bigwigs* challenge!"

Vivi looked confused. "What do you mean, 'again'?" she asked Delilah.

"We were filming a little segment of Jack 'out and about' yesterday," said Delilah. "We'd already got some great footage of Jack's famous bachelor pad, but—"

"Bachelor pad?" said Vivi and Darylyn. Reese and Sampson cast skeptical looks at each other.

Jack looked at them as though they were crazy.

"You know. My bachelor pad. The one I've been . . . doing all my bachelor business in." His voice sounded regrettably high.

He cleared his throat and glanced nervously at the camera, checking that the red light was off.

"You can't be a bachelor," Darylyn said. "Technically a bachelor's someone who's old enough to get married but deliberately chooses not to."

"Whatever," said Jack. "The point is, it's mine."

"I don't get it," said Vivi. "How can you even afford that? I thought you'd spent all your—oh. Wait. I get it. This 'bachelor pad': It wouldn't be situated a few yards from the back door of your house, by any chance?"

"Maybe," said Jack.

"So we're talking less 'bachelor pad' and more . . . 'bungalow'?"

Out of the corner of his eye, Jack saw Sampson shaking his head in pity.

Delilah checked her watch. "So, what I'd really like to do is get some shots of Jack hanging out with his friends before school starts. All five of you."

"Four," said Jack.

Delilah looked confused. Reese nudged Jack, nodding toward Sampson. "Dude."

"Okay," Jack sighed. "Whatever. Five."

"Great," said Delilah. "Maybe you could talk a little about what it's like to hang out with a Bigwig, what's happening at school today, that kind of thing."

Darylyn fixed Delilah with a serious stare. "That sounds completely stilted and unnatural," she said. And then, after a micro-pause, "Fortunately, that is one hundred percent my bag."

"Great," said Delilah, looking slightly unsure. She moved Brett into place and Todd positioned his mike above them, out of shot.

A crowd was starting to gather along the fence, inside

the school grounds. Jack spied the seventh-grade girls kneeling down at the front, hands gripping the wire, rigid with excitement.

When nobody seemed willing to start talking, Delilah turned to Jack. "Okay. Here's an icebreaker. How does a typical school day compare to a typical day on *Bigwigs*? What's on the timetable for Monday?"

Sampson butted in before Jack could answer. "We have PE in the afternoon. Don't we, Jack?"

"Do we? I can't remember," Jack countered with a shrug. "I've got a lot on my mind right now. You know, with all this *Bigwigs* reunion show stuff happening."

Sampson put on a look of mock concern and turned to Delilah.

"You're not taking the camera into the locker room, I hope."

Delilah blanched. "Of course not," she said. "That would be totally inappropriate."

"Good," said Sampson. "It's just that some of the guys are . . . well, not *all* the way to becoming actual *guys*, if you know what I mean. Could be a bit embarrassing for them. But we're playing soccer again this afternoon. You could film that! Jack might even save a goal this time."

Jack shrugged. "Film it if you want." (He definitely did not want them to film it.) "But I'm not really into games. I mean, that sort of thing's fine if you're in sixth grade or whatever." He cleared his throat in what he hoped was a manful way. "Obviously I pursue more mature interests these days."

"Oh?" said Delilah. "Such as?"

Vivi pretended to be intrigued. "Yes, Jack. Tell us about all these manly pursuits. Are they the kinds of things that would keep you holed up in your bedroom—sorry, *bachelor pad*—for two whole weeks?"

Darylyn leaned toward Delilah. "Jack has been 'exploring himself.'"

Reese nudged Darylyn. "Dude! *Ix-nay* on the *asturbating-may*!" he whispered out the side of his mouth. He looked like he was struggling to suppress a grin.

"What are you even talking about?" said Jack. "*Yes*, I've been exploring myself. *No*, not in *that* way. More like . . . getting in touch with my inner animal."

"Yeah," said Sampson. "The chipmunk."

"It's not a chipmunk," said Jack, scowling. "It's a man animal. An inner man animal."

Delilah's searchlight stare flicked from Jack to Vivi to Sampson and back to Jack again.

"So tell us more," she said. "What kind of manly things are we talking about here?"

"Well . . . ," said Jack, delaying for a moment as he struggled to think of something plausible. He thought about the Lionheart Tigerwolf thing Mr. Trench had told him about. At the time he thought it sounded ridiculous; now he was desperate enough to reach for it like a lifeline. Jack set his jaw firm and did his best to look grim and serious. "Well, obviously there's my hunting."

Sampson made a *pfft* noise. Vivi rolled her eyes.

"I mean, not *hunting* hunting, like, with spears or anything. But, you know. Shooting. Firing guns at things."

Reese and Darylyn looked at each other, frowning.

"Yeah, I've been spending quite a lot of time down at the rifle range with the guys. The old shootin' gang. Fishing I like, also," said Jack. "Love catching a fish. Gutting a fish. Skinning a fish. And then there's my boxing, of course."

Dammit, he thought. Why had he said boxing? It was *wrestling* that Mr. Trench had mentioned, he remembered. A combat sport that involved considerably less chance of having your face punched in.

"When I say boxing, I mean boxing-themed gym workout," he added, quickly saving himself. "I work out with a punching bag." He did a couple of swift jabs for the camera, then immediately stopped when he realized how ridiculous he looked. "So, yeah. Fishing. Shooting. Fish . . . shooting."

"Fish *punching*?" suggested Vivi innocently.

Jack nodded, looking serious, as though weighed down by some enormous duty. "If it comes to it."

"We love you, Jack!" shouted the seventh-grade girls.

Delilah glanced over toward where the girls had gathered, under the birch tree near the fence. They seemed to have pinged Delilah's radar—but before she could quiz Jack for information, the bell rang.

"Okay, we might wrap there for now," she said. "I think you're right, Jack. It sounds like we'll get more interesting material outside of school hours."

"Really?" said Jack. "That's it?" He tried not to sound too relieved.

Delilah nodded and turned to Brett, who handed her the blue folder from his bag. She handed release forms to Vivi, Reese, and Darylyn, then spoke to Jack again. "I'm going to extend our shoot. So we can get some footage of you doing all those things you were just talking about."

"Brilliant," said Jack. "Good plan."

On the one hand, the less filming at school, the better. On the other hand, all the interesting things he'd just talked about were 100 percent bogus. He'd never fired a gun, he'd never caught a fish, and he'd never thrown a punch.

How the hell was he going to fake *that*?

Chapter Eighteen

he crew had piled their gear back into the van. "I'll be in touch soon," Delilah promised Jack. She climbed into the front passenger seat, and a moment later the van was gone.

The crowd that had gathered to watch the filming began to roll slowly into school. Glances were cast back at Jack. He heard people whisper the words "Jack Sprigley" and "reunion episode." The seventh-grade girls jumped up and down, clutching one another as they scurried away to homeroom, like they needed to be physically convinced of the miraculous event that had just taken place before them.

"So that was us, being filmed for TV," said Darylyn. She

nudged Reese. "I'm prepared to bet you'll look even more handsome on TV than you do in real life."

Reese smirked, then glanced awkwardly at Jack.

Vivi held out her release form. Along with the forms, Delilah had given them each a stamped envelope already addressed to the *Bigwigs* production office. "What are they going to do if my parents don't sign this?"

"They'll probably just pixelate your face," said Sampson. "That happens sometimes. Though I've never heard of them doing it on *Bigwigs*." He paused. "Not that I'm an expert."

Vivi gave Sampson a puzzled look, then led the way into school. Reese hung back, letting Vivi and Sampson and Darylyn get a little ahead. He turned to Jack.

"Why are you doing this, dude?"

"Doing what?"

"All this big-talking yourself in front of the camera. You never did that the first time you were on *Bigwigs*. I've seen the clips. And what have you got *against fish* all of a sudden?"

Jack shrugged. "Things aren't the same as when I was on *Bigwigs* the first time. Things are different now."

Reese looked away. "Dude, I don't know what to say. I'm *sorry* things have changed, okay? I feel crappy about it. But it wasn't *planned*, you know? It just happened. Like, nine years of knowing each other and suddenly it's like, 'Dude!

You're awesomeness in girl form!'" He paused. "Hey, why am *I* saying sorry?"

"You think this is all because of you and Darylyn?"

Reese shrugged. "Isn't it?"

Jack sighed as Reese put his earbuds back in. Reese was right: He didn't need to apologize. It wasn't Reese's fault that Jack was slowly but surely humiliating himself in front of the *Bigwigs* cameras. It wasn't Darylyn's fault either, or Vivi's, even though she'd brought Sampson into the group. (He decided it was at least partly Sampson's fault—just because.)

But one thing was certain: His return to *Bigwigs* was *not* working out the way he'd hoped.

"Maybe you were right," said Jack. "Maybe I'm not ready for this. Maybe I *don't* belong back on *Bigwigs*."

Jack looked ahead and saw Vivi swat Sampson with her rolled-up release form. Apparently he had just said something super hilarious.

Reese pulled out his right earbud. "What did you say?"

Jack stared ahead at Vivi and Sampson. "I said, maybe I don't belong."

The news that a TV crew had been filming near the main gates swept through Upland Junior High. At an assembly that morning, Principal Byrne explained that, yes, the *Bigwigs* producers had sought permission to film at the school, but that no firm plans were in place.

"So you can hold off on those dreams of hitting the big time, just for now," she added.

Jack spent the rest of the day feeling watched. His first day as a seventh grader had been exactly the same. He'd come to junior high fresh from *Bigwigs*, and spent the whole of that first morning trying to get away from the starstruck stares and envious scowls.

And then there they'd been, hanging around just inside the school gate. Vivi: strawberry-blond, leaning against the fence, bright blue eyes shaded by a huge floppy sun hat. Darylyn: small, dark haired, standing motionless like a startled bird. Reese: plugged into his music player, Afro hair shaped into a fauxhawk. All three of them had looked back at him with a complete lack of recognition or curiosity.

As if they hadn't known who he was.

Jack hadn't been able to stop the grin from spreading across his face.

"Hi," he'd said. "I'm Jack."

After that, Jack had forgotten all about *Bigwigs*. So had everyone else, eventually—with the exception of a certain trio of seventh-grade girls. And a certain Oliver Sampson.

Things were great—for a while. Now everything was weird and different. Things were *complicated*.

The big time, thought Jack.

Faking it was turning out to be harder than he'd thought.

The Boulevard Motel was one of about a dozen motels and miniresorts that lined the main highway into town. The classier ones were all built and owned by the Bruno Distagio property development empire.

This was not one of the classier ones.

Jack spotted the minivan right away. He leaned his bike against the wall of the reception building, crossed the car park to room fourteen, and knocked on the door.

Delilah was busy on the phone when she answered. She mouthed a *"Hi!"* and waved Jack in. It looked like she hadn't got around to completely unpacking her suitcase yet. A laptop was open on the bench next to the bar fridge. *The Bold and the Beautiful* was on the TV. Jack figured Brett and Todd had their own rooms. He wondered if they were watching *The Bold and the Beautiful* too, and decided it was unlikely.

He was glad Delilah was alone. He didn't want anyone else hearing what he was about to confess.

Delilah wrapped up her call with a string of "Okays," then tossed the phone aside and turned to Jack. "Hi, Jack. What's all this about wanting to come clean?"

Jack took a deep breath and plunged in before he had a chance to rethink his decision. "I'm just in kind of a weird place at the moment, and I guess I've been saying a few things lately that . . . aren't exactly true?"

"Okay . . . ," said Delilah.

"Like, today, what I said about the shooting and the fishing and the boxing and everything? Well . . . none of it's real. I . . . made it up."

Delilah looked not entirely amazed. Jack wasn't sure what he'd been hoping to achieve by telling her. Maybe he just felt guilty. Maybe he was hoping she'd offer to scrap what they'd filmed and start again. He thought there was a good chance she'd chew him out for being unprofessional. He remembered seeing an executive on *Bigwigs* throwing a tantrum at an intern, the first week of filming, for not being able to get celebrity chef Courtnee Devries to the location for Blue Team's restaurant challenge because of a grounded plane. The executive had gone red in the face and screamed, "Fix it! Just fix it! Do you think *my* boss would just accept it if I wobbled my lip and said, 'But I have no influence over air safety regulations'? No! So *fix it!*"

But Delilah didn't yell or scream. She just nodded slowly, thinking for a moment. "I'm glad you told me. I was starting to worry about this whole shoot."

"What do you mean?"

"This is reality TV, Jack. The last thing we want you to be is *yourself.*"

Jack was surprised at how much that sentence seemed to make sense.

"Actually, I'm glad you're bringing these ideas to the table," said Delilah. "It gives us something to work with. So let me get this straight: You're telling me that all those things you mentioned today—the shooting, the fishing, the boxing—they're not real?"

Jack nodded.

"Okay. My question is: Do you want them to be?"

Chapter Nineteen

~~~~~~

Jack blinked, swallowed—and squeezed the trigger.

A muffled crack split the air. The rifle butt dug hard into his shoulder, even through the padding he was wearing.

Jack squinted through his protective goggles, then turned to look behind him. "Did I hit anything?"

The range officer for the Upland Rifle Club stood huddled with Delilah and the crew at the back of Jack's firing lane. There were a dozen other lanes in the concrete enclosure, which sat in the middle of a fifty-acre patch of scrub just outside town. The range officer raised his binoculars, paused for a moment, then turned to Delilah, shaking his head.

"Doesn't matter!" Delilah shouted back. She leaned over to talk to Brett, who pried one of his earmuffs away from his head to hear what she was saying.

Jack went to remove his own earmuffs, but the range officer held up a cautioning finger and pointed to the open grassy area next to the enclosure. Jack looked over and saw two shooters lying on their stomachs on the grass, their rifles aimed at the targets. One was a kid around Jack's age. He figured the other shooter was the kid's dad.

When Jack looked closer, he realized the kid was Kenny Hodgman; the second-to-last boy to grow pubes in eighth grade. He'd had no idea the Hodgemeister was a shooter. Maybe that was how he'd finally kick-started puberty into action—by taking up the rifle, just like Jack was doing.

Jack wondered if Sampson had ever fired a gun. Knowing him, he probably had a bazooka at home.

"A few more rounds for the camera, Jack!" shouted Delilah. She mimed shooting an invisible rifle at random points in the air. Jack couldn't tell, because of the earmuffs, but he was fairly sure she was making shooty noises out the side of her mouth.

Jack turned back to the bench rest where the .22 rifle had been set up for him. He nestled the butt of the rifle firmly into his shoulder, where the padding on his rented shooting vest was thickest, the way the range officer had shown him.

He fired three more shots, then turned to Delilah again. "I still don't think I hit anything!"

A series of shots rang out from the grassy area next to the enclosure. Delilah made a "time out" sign, then touched the range officer's shoulder and asked him something. He nodded and sent two of his staff off to opposite ends of the enclosure.

"Just calling a cease-fire," Delilah announced as she took off her earmuffs. Jack noticed that Brett had gone around the back of the enclosure and was climbing into a Jeep with one of the range staff. "Don't want my only cameraman coming back looking like Swiss cheese!" she joked.

The range officer and Todd laughed.

"Yeah," said Jack. "Like, imagine if someone accidentally shot the cameraman and he died!"

Silence.

The range officer emptied Jack's rifle of ammo and helped him out of the shooting vest. "That was a good first time, son. A lot of boys your age can't handle the recoil."

Jack wondered how old the range officer thought he was.

The Jeep had pulled up next to the sandbag backstops piled behind the targets at the far end of the range. Jack saw Brett jump out of the Jeep, camera on his shoulder.

"How did that feel?" Delilah asked, as the range officer took Jack's goggles and earmuffs and laid them onto the folded vest.

"Okay," said Jack. "I wish I'd actually hit a target. I guess I showed those sandbags a thing or two, though."

Delilah shrugged. "You looked like a natural. It'll make great TV."

When Brett returned, driven back to the enclosure in the Jeep, Jack asked to see what he'd filmed. The cameraman glanced at Delilah, who nodded.

Jack leaned over and peered into the viewfinder as Brett scrolled back through his footage. The screen froze on a shot of one of the targets, with two ragged holes inside the eight ring, and one inside the nine ring, close to the bull's-eye.

He glanced over at the grassy area next to the enclosure, where Kenny Hodgman was getting ready to fire again now that the range was clear.

"All good?" asked Delilah.

Jack nodded. "Yeah," he said. "All good."

The instructor cast the line into the water and passed the rod to Jack. Jack had finally gotten used to the boat lurching every time the instructor leaned over to grab some fresh bait or check one of the rods. Even so, he was glad to be wearing the flotation vest.

Jack glanced over at Delilah, who stood on the riverbank with the crew. At her feet was a small blue cooler she'd had with her when they'd collected Jack at sunrise. When he'd asked her what was in it, all she'd said was "coverage." She didn't elaborate.

Jack had never been out on the Redcook River—not even on one of the paddle steamers that chugged tourists up and down the river for most of the year. He'd swum at its edges with elementary-school friends during summer break, and played baseball on the sandbar near the trailer park upstream.

Out on the river itself, the stillness was eerie. Jack lost all sense of time. Occasionally he caught the fishing instructor just staring at the water. Maybe the instructor saw some mysterious pattern in the ripples left by the bugs as they skimmed the surface. Maybe he saw some hidden truth in the murky depths that Jack couldn't.

Jack stared broodingly at the water. He wondered if Sampson had ever caught a fish. (*"Does wrestling a shark count?"* he'd probably say.) He hoped the camera was capturing his now very profound understanding of all things natural. His ease with the elements. His Lionheart Tigerwolfiness.

He'd actually considered letting Delilah know about Mr. Trench and his weird wilderness survival group, in case they could help out with the fishing or shooting segments. But then he'd had visions of Mr. Trench paddling over to him in a camouflage-painted dinghy, with lures and spinners stuck into the band of his fishing hat like ammunition on a bandolier, and announcing on camera how proud he was of Jack for finally becoming the "commanding officer of his Y chromosome" or something equally ridiculous. Mr. Trench had way too much embarrassing intel on Jack and his testosterone troubles to be let anywhere near the *Bigwigs* cameras.

Anyway, it was actually Delilah making the whole manhood thing happen. She was doing a way better job of faking manhood for Jack than he ever could have managed on his own.

"Any luck?" Delilah shouted from the riverbank.

The fisherman nudged Jack. "She'd be scaring the fish away, shouting like that. That's if there were any fish to catch." He gave Jack an apologetic look. "They're just not biting today, son."

"We've got nothing!" Jack shouted back.

Delilah held up a hand and knelt down to open the cooler. She reached in and pulled out a slim, greeny-yellow fish. She handed it to Todd, then wiped her hands on the back of her skirt.

"Yellowbelly," said the fisherman.

"What?" said Jack.

"That's a golden perch. A yellowbelly. She's gone and bought you your catch."

Jack realized what it was. A stunt fish. The fisherman

raised his eyebrows at Jack but said nothing. He gave the outboard motor a yank and aimed the boat for the riverbank, where Todd was edging his way toward the water, holding forth the fish like some kind of sacred offering.

As the boat got nearer, Jack reached out to grab the fish. But just as the fake catch was within reach, Todd slipped. He skidded down the bank and tumbled sideways into the river.

The fish fell out of his hands, landed in the water with a plop, and immediately sank.

Todd was chest-deep in water and didn't look particularly happy about it. In fact, the string of words he let out through chattering teeth was guaranteed to have frightened any fish that might have heard them. Even the fishing instructor seemed slightly taken aback.

"Are you okay?" said Jack.

Todd didn't answer. He pulled himself out of the river and seemed to be doing his best not to shiver. Muddy water dripped from his beard. He continued to not look particularly happy.

"Did we lose the fish?" asked Delilah.

Jack nodded. "What are we going to do now?" he asked.

"It's okay," said Delilah. "We got some shots of you in the boat. With the right voice-over, I'm sure we can sell the whole 'rugged outdoorsman' concept." She checked her watch. "Okay, Fisherman Jack, we'd better get you to school!

Tomorrow afternoon we hit the gym." She faked an upper-cut jab and made a *pow!* noise.

The gym, thought Jack. Where there'd be no shooting vests or flotation vests to protect him. He pictured the shots of him in shorts and a tank top, landing feeble blows against a punching bag.

He pictured himself in the locker room, getting ready.

And he pictured Oliver Sampson standing there in front of him, laughing.

Chapter Twenty

Jack stared at himself in the bathroom mirror. He held his skinny bare arms out in front of himself, and wondered if Delilah could buy him some muscle powder from the drugstore, to really complete his on-screen transformation.

She kept telling him how great the firing range and fishing boat stuff was going to look on TV. And he did *feel* different, somehow. When he'd laid hands on the rifle and the fishing rod, it felt a bit like taking hold of a flame passed down to him by the earliest, manliest cavemen. The problem was that it was all on the inside. Nobody watching the reunion show was going to notice *that*.

Maybe it was time to get that tattoo he'd been thinking about. A rifle and fishing rod, crossed like clashing swords. Or "wig" on the knuckles of one hand, and "big" on the other. Something to distract everyone from the tragic shortage of biceps and body hair his tank top and gym shorts were guaranteed to reveal.

Tracksuit, he thought. *Tracksuit bottom and hoodie.* A fleecy armor to hide inside. He'd be like a warrior in a sheepskin cloak. Let the *Bigwigs* viewers *imagine* the rippling, muscular powerhouse underneath.

Jack opened his chest of drawers and rummaged through the piles of clothes Philo had stashed away for him during the move.

And that was when he saw it. The thing that kept following him around, finding its way back to him.

Like Samwise Gamgee from *The Lord of the Rings*, but made of pubes.

There was one other difference between Sam Gamgee and Philo's merkin. Frodo Baggins *needed* Sam. Jack most definitely did not need—

Then he thought for a moment. And he thought for a moment longer. Then, after a further moment of thought, he reached in, fingers like forceps, and extracted the merkin from the drawer.

With a quick glance over his shoulder to check that

nobody was about to walk in on him, Jack padded back into the bathroom and stood in front of the mirror. With one hand he dangled the merkin out in front of him, and with the other, he tugged down the neck of his tank top to bare his hairless chest.

Could he? Would it be too obvious? Too up-front? He cocked his head and squinted as he draped the merkin across his pectorals, trying to imagine how it would look on camera.

Probably how it looks in the mirror, he thought.

Like pubes.

Maybe there were other options. Less visible options. Options that would still give off an overall impression of manliness.

He peeled the merkin from his chest, lifted one arm in the air, and inched the wiry black thatch tentatively toward his armpit. If he cut the merkin in half—

"Jack?"

He spun around to see his mom standing in the bungalow doorway. "Mom!" He whisked the merkin behind his back. "Some privacy, please! I'm . . . *rehearsing*!"

"Pardon me, Mr. De Niro!" Adele craned her neck slightly, as if she were trying to see over Jack's shoulder. "I thought you should know. Delilah just called. She wants to come over."

Jack frowned. "What, tonight? Why?"

"Something about a change of plans? It sounds urgent."

Jack wondered what it could have been. Had Kenny Hodgman blabbed to the press about being the one to hit bull's-eye instead of Jack? Had the media got hold of the "fake fish" story?

Calm down, thought Jack. A change of plans, his mom had said. "Maybe we're not filming at the gym tomorrow after all," he wondered aloud, trying his best to sound disappointed.

Adele looked doubtful. "I think it might be bigger than that. She said something about rethinking the whole reunion show."

Behind his back, Jack clenched both his hands, giving the merkin an anxious squeeze. Did rethinking the reunion show mean what he thought it meant? Was *Bigwigs* about to be taken away from him again? Sampson would have a field day with *that* news. He realized how tightly he was clutching the merkin. He wanted to fling it away, but his mom was still standing in the doorway.

"Oh! I forgot to tell you, Philo stopped by earlier in the week while you were out with Delilah. He said he had something he wanted to drop off for you?"

Jack went pale. Had Philo made another merkin? A second-generation model with twice the sticking power and double the pubes? He'd been cagey about what he'd been researching when Jack had found him in the library, but he'd insisted it wasn't another merkin. So what *was* it? With Philo's track record, it was guaranteed to be *massively* embarrassing. After all, Philo had started off with fake pubes. The next logical step was . . .

Oh my God, thought Jack. *It's going to be fake junk.* He had a vision of a huge papier-mâché dong springing out from a drawer like something from an X-rated pop-up book. But surely his mom would have noticed Philo walking *that* through the house?

"This thing Philo dropped off," Jack said, trying to sound calmer than he felt. "Was it big? Was it small?"

Adele shook her head. "I was on my way out to work. I wasn't really paying attention." She frowned. "What's the matter? You're acting like he's hidden a snake in your room or something."

A trouser-snake, maybe, thought Jack darkly. "It's okay," he said. "I'll just . . . finish up here, then I'll come in for dinner."

Adele craned her neck again, obviously hoping for a glimpse of whatever Jack was holding behind his back. Luckily, Jack's body seemed to be blocking the reflection of his merkin-clutching hands in the bathroom mirror.

"Okay," said his mom, pausing at the door on her way out. "You'll never guess what we're having."

"Great," said Hallie. "Sausages again. I'll pass."

Jack drummed his fingers nervously on the kitchen table. As soon as his mom had left, he'd upturned his entire bachelor pad. He yanked out drawers and flung T-shirts and socks and underpants over his shoulder in a desperate search for Philo's new pube-prop.

Nothing. His room was a mess, and he'd found nothing.

Philo must have suffered one of his typical brain-fades and had forgotten to actually leave the mystery item for Jack to find. It was the only explanation Jack could come up with.

"When did Delilah say she's coming?"

"Soon," said Adele from the kitchen. She rolled another spatula-load of sausages onto a plate.

Marlene looked up from her phone. "I'd like to be excused, if it's all the same to everyone. The whole house feels like it's under bloomin' surveillance. I had to shoo three *very* peculiar young ladies off the front lawn the other afternoon."

Hallie threw a look at Jack. "Yeah, and Nats won't stop going on about *Bigwigs* being in town. Yaz and Stace are getting super bitchy about it and blaming *me*."

"I get it," Jack said, rolling his eyes at his sister. "I'm the worst. Anyway, it sounds like this whole *Bigwigs* reunion thing's going to be canceled anyway. That's probably my fault too, for not being a big exciting celebrity like all the other contestants. So that's good news for you."

"We don't *know* that it's going to be canceled," said Adele. "Let's wait and see what Delilah says before we go overreacting."

Marlene leaned over to Jack and touched his arm. "I don't mean to be such a grouch, Jack. I'm just having a little trouble controlling my temper at the moment. And you know, I have been evicted from my own bungalow and so forth."

Jack felt Marlene's grip on his arm get tighter and tighter. It was alarmingly strong, as though he were being pawed at by an angry gorilla and not a seventy-year-old woman. She didn't seem to realize she was doing it; she just kept smiling sweetly at him as she applied more and more pressure. "Anyway, hopefully everything will be back to normal soon," she continued. "That'll be nice, won't it, Jack?"

As she spoke, her voice suddenly pitched downward, as though it had been treated with some kind of demonic Auto-Tune. At first Jack thought she was making fun of him, deepening her voice to sound like the man that Jack definitely wasn't. But then he saw the look of shock and embarrassment on her face.

Hallie had heard it too. She shot Jack a "What the hell was that?" glance.

The only person who hadn't heard it was Adele, who was busy dousing the greasy frying pan in soapy dishwater.

Jack felt the blood rushing back to his arm as Marlene released her grip and retreated into awkward silence.

Adele carried the sausages to the table. "Everyone's gone very quiet," she observed.

"Just . . . in awe of tonight's tower of sausage," said Hallie, eyes still wide with alarm.

"Y-yeah," said Jack. He clasped his hands together and bowed his head. "We give you thanks, Almighty Lord, for these almighty sausages. . . ."

As he made the pretend prayer, he wondered if he should mention something about his gran apparently being possessed by Satan.

Jack was halfway through the first of his four sausages when the doorbell rang.

"I'm really sorry to interrupt your dinner," said Delilah, as Adele welcomed her in. She nodded toward the table. "Still getting through those sausages, I see."

"Only a pound to go," said Adele. "How's the filming going? Jack's being very tight-lipped about it all."

Hallie and Marlene took the opportunity to make their exit.

Delilah looked distracted. "The filming? It's going great. Jack's segment's certainly going to be . . . different."

Jack was relieved. Unless he was imagining things, it didn't sound like the show was being canceled after all. "Different, but still 'as good as,' right?"

"You're talking about it as though it's still a competition . . . ," said his mom warily.

"Actually, that's exactly what I wanted to talk to you about," Delilah cut in excitedly. "There's an idea I've been pitching to the execs. It's been on my mind ever since we started talking about this reunion special. A fresh angle. Something that takes the episode to a whole new level."

Something about the way Delilah was speaking took Jack back to when he was twelve again, during the first week of the *Bigwigs* finals. He and Hope Chanders had been pitted against each other in a challenge to produce a ringtone that viewers could download. He remembered sitting there, just before the recording of the results show, listening to the producers explaining exactly how the *Bigwigs* finals were going to pan out. A cold, constricted feeling grew in his stomach.

"What I want to do—what the whole *team* wants to do—is make this reunion more of a *contest*. Sure, everyone's going to tune in to see the new batch of Bigwigs, and they'll be curious to see the original contestants come back on the show for a lap of honor. That's all great. But what if we could give them something more? These packages we're doing: What if they're not just little 'Where are they now?' segments? What if they were more like *auditions*?"

"Auditions for what?" said Adele.

Delilah looked like a proud parent. "For a permanent spot on the Bigwigs Board." She caught Jack's eye. "A regular, paying gig as a full-time cast member."

Jack's apprehension turned to nervous excitement. The Bigwigs Board was the judging panel that decided each week who would stay and who would go. It was a massive responsibility. Jack would basically decide the fate of the next batch of contestants. It wouldn't be just a one-off reunion appearance. There was a chance that *Bigwigs* might want him back *for good.*

Sampson would absolutely *spew* if he had to watch Jack on the show every single week.

Plus, Jack liked how it sounded. *Bigwigs Board member.* It had a certain manly gravitas to it.

"I don't know," said Adele. "That's a much bigger deal than just going back for a reunion. . . ."

"You're right," said Delilah. "It *is* a much bigger deal. What do you think, Jack? The segments we're filming, they'll have to show everyone why you'd be a good choice for the Bigwigs Board. They'll need to show you can be a leader, that you can make the tough decisions like sending contestants home. That you're comfortable with that kind of power."

Jack stared down at his plate of sausages. So far all he'd proved was that he could hit a target (not really) and catch a fish (not really). But Delilah seemed to be on his side. She'd masterminded the firing range and the fishing boat. She'd given him a masculinity makeover for the cameras. She'd done her best to turn him into the man he kept telling everyone he was.

Now he needed to prove he had what it took to be a Bigwigs Board member. And it had just occurred to Jack that there was a perfect opportunity to demonstrate his leadership skills right there for the taking. The more he thought about it, the more perfect it seemed. The *Bigwigs* producers wouldn't be able to refuse him the position. Not after Delilah turned him into the biggest man in town.

For a week.

Chapter Twenty-One

The junior mayoral robes had obviously been designed for someone bigger. Jack felt like an impostor in fancy dress as Mayor Neville Perry-Moore helped Jack slip the ceremonial gold chain and medallion over his head.

Mayor Perry-Moore seemed smaller and grayer than Jack remembered him being when they'd stood side by side at the opening of the Upland South Childcare Center. Even so, it was obvious why people had voted him in as mayor five times in a row. It wasn't just his experience and his silver-fox good looks. It wasn't even that he was so devoted to Upland that he'd never married. No, the real reason that Mayor Perry-Moore was so popular was that he somehow managed to make you in awe of his power while at the same time making you feel like he was your best friend.

Jack tried to remember the last time he felt like anyone's best friend. After what he'd just done, it wasn't a feeling he was likely to recapture anytime soon.

Mayor Perry-Moore stepped to one side and put his hand on Jack's shoulder. "I hereby invest you, Jack Sprigley, with this chain of office, and pronounce you the City of Upland's newest Mayor for a Week."

There was a smattering of applause from the gathered witnesses in the council office. Jack's mom sat in the front row with Reese, Darylyn, and Philo. Reese huddled toward Darylyn, away from Philo's overenthusiastic clapping. Delilah and her crew were at the back of the room, camera rolling. The three seventh-grade girls were at the back too, jumping up and down on the spot and waving JACK IS BACK signs. A reporter from the *Upland Daily* stood to the side, taking notes, while a photographer knelt in the aisle and took shots of Jack shaking Mayor Perry-Moore's hand. The rest of the audience was made up of Mr. Jacobs and Ms. Liaw, and a handful of the other candidates who'd applied to be Mayor for a Week.

Not that Jack had actually *applied*, as such. Not technically.

Mayor Perry-Moore waited patiently for the seventh-grade girls to shift gears down from wild, hysterical excitement to merely hysterical excitement.

"Now, before we hear a few words from our new Mayor

for a Week, I want to mention the special circumstances of this year's Mayor for a Week program. This year, Jack will be serving in office for the launch of the Fourteenth Annual Upland Hot-Air Balloon Festival. I'm entrusting our new Mayor for a Week with the responsibility of representing me in the traditional Mayor's Balloon Race." Mayor Perry-Moore placed a hand lightly on Jack's back. "I hope you're not afraid of heights, Jack." He chuckled.

"Heights?" Jack glanced at the *Bigwigs* camera. The red light was on. He hoped he looked bigger than he felt, buried under the swathes of royal blue cotton. This was it. His audition for the Bigwigs Board had begun.

"Heights are not a problem. Definitely no problem with heights. Reaching them, or . . . being at them. In fact, I look forward to reaching new *heights* of excellence"—he resisted the urge to wink at the camera—"in the field of being a mayor."

Jack could sense the groan about to escape from Vivi before it actually came. He guessed she'd been holding on to it for a while, having been standing next to Jack for so long, waiting her turn.

The mayor beckoned for Vivi to come closer. "There's another reason why this is such a special year. Owing to the outstanding quality of entries, we've decided, for the first time ever, to appoint a *Deputy* Mayor for a Week. And the bearer of this inaugural office, I'm *very* pleased to announce, is Miss Vivi Dink-Dawson."

There was a much healthier round of applause—and a noticeable lack of sign-waving from the seventh-grade girls. Vivi stepped forward.

Mayor Perry-Moore looked apologetic as he shook Vivi's hand. "I'm afraid we haven't got any deputy mayoral robes to give you. This is a rather . . . unique situation."

Vivi shook her head. "It's okay. Obviously, I would have been honored to wear the robes and chain. After all," she added, glancing at Jack, "I do love me some civic regalia. But it's not the clothes that maketh the mayor. It's ideas. Passion. Integrity."

"Well, I think everyone on the council would agree that your application spoke volumes about your passion and integrity," said Mayor Perry-Moore.

Standing off to the side of the presentation area was the woman from the council who'd spoken at the Mayor for a Week information session at school. Jack saw her smile warmly at Vivi. Then she noticed Jack looking at her, and the smile faded.

"Well," said Vivi, "as I put forth in my essay—because I actually *did* write an essay—I'm especially passionate about finding a balance between building Upland's economy and preserving the environment. For instance, how many more riverside resorts does the Distagio family really need to build?" She turned to Jack. "Hopefully the Mayor for a Week and I share some common policy ground there."

Jack coughed nervously. He didn't have any policies, as such. There hadn't been time. Delilah had swung into action as soon as Jack had pitched the idea to her, pulling strings and making deals to get Jack named Mayor for a Week ahead of all the *real* candidates.

The camera was still rolling. He never knew a black chunk of plastic and glass could look so *expectant*. He was going to have to improvise—in a way he hadn't had to do since *Bigwigs*. And it had to be convincing enough to show everyone he had what it took to be on the Bigwigs Board.

"Totally," he said. "I mean . . . I think the environment's super important too. I look forward to discussing the issues with Miss Dink-Dawson over the coming week." Jack caught Vivi's eye and held it. He tried to convey an "I'm sorry, I wouldn't do this if I didn't have to" look to her.

The look she gave him back was even worse than the stare of the camera lens.

A buffet had been set up in one corner of the room. Jack did his best to avoid Vivi and the others as he navigated the small crowd in search of a paper cup of weak lemonade.

Yes, technically he'd cheated. Worse, he'd gotten someone

else to do the actual cheating for him. But he *had* suggested that Vivi could be his deputy. Surely that had to count for something.

He could hear Delilah giving a spiel to the newspaper reporter. "Yes, we've had a *very* warm welcome from everyone in Upland, and we're really looking forward to filming Jack's big moment as stand-in mayor at the balloon festival. It will show our viewers what a Bigwig can become. And it will show off Upland to the rest of the country. Everyone tuning in for the season-opening reunion special—airing on Family Network in two weeks, write that down—will see firsthand what a remarkable place Upland really is."

The reporter thanked Delilah and went off in search of sustenance at the buffet, where her photographer was already munching on his fourth sushi roll.

"You're pretty good at all this PR stuff," said Jack.

"That's five years at the country's top drama school for you," muttered Delilah. "Listen, do you think you can round up your friends for me? We need to get some footage of Jack Sprigley's new crew."

It was Delilah's idea to get Jack's friends to design the hot-air balloon Jack was going to fly in for the opening-night race. Delilah had found a manufacturer who could sew and deliver a balloon at short notice. They'd sent her a template, and Delilah had paid for a 3-D-modeling program for Darylyn's laptop.

Jack had recommended bringing Philo on board for his design skills, though Jack didn't elaborate on how he'd discovered them. He figured it would be a good way to keep Philo occupied for the next week, so he didn't come up with any more surprise "gifts" for Jack. Plus, it made the team just big enough that there was no room for Oliver Sampson to shoulder his way in.

Jack sidled over to the buffet, where Reese, Darylyn, and Philo were comparing notes on the platter of cupcakes. Vivi was at the other end of the buffet, deep in conversation with the mayor.

"Um, guys? Delilah wants the gang together for the cameras."

Reese and Darylyn exchanged glances. *"The gang,"* Reese silently mouthed. Still, they filed over obediently to where Delilah and her crew were standing. Jack grabbed Philo's elbow as he followed after them.

"Hey, I've been meaning to ask. What was this thing you left in my bachelor pad?" he whispered.

Philo looked blankly back at him. "I didn't leave anything in your bachelor pad."

"Are you sure? Mom said you came over and left something in the bungalow."

Philo shook his head. "I . . . definitely did not leave anything in the bungalow. . . ."

Jack was relieved. He figured his first instinct was right: Philo had spaced out and completely forgotten to leave behind whatever it was he'd brought over.

Delilah hustled Philo, Darylyn, and Reese in front of the camera. "Okay, so imagine we have a voice-over here saying something about—Philo, was it?—Philo being Mr. Designer Guy, and Darylyn being the 3-D whiz, and Reese—" She paused. "What's Reese's job?"

Reese scowled. "Moral support."

Delilah nodded. "Great. Let's get some footage of you three singing the praises of your glorious leader."

Reese and Darylyn stared at each other. "Jack's not our leader," said Darylyn, direct to camera.

Reese shot Jack a look. "We just hang out."

Yeah, thought Jack. *When you remember to. When you're not too busy having girlfriends and getting pimples and pubes.*

Philo's face lit up. "I can tell you something about Jack! Something very few people know!"

Jack's blood froze. He tried to get Philo's attention, but it was too late.

"Jack was once a contestant on a reality show! On TV! It was called *Bigwigs*."

Delilah looked alarmed. "You do know that *we're* from *Bigwigs*?" She gestured back at the cameraman and sound guy. "You do realize we're filming for *Bigwigs* right now?"

"I don't think it's a very good idea calling your show *Bigwigs*, just between us." Philo mimed holding a phone to his ear. "Hello, is this the copycat police? I want to report a copycat." He paused. "Yes, I'll hold."

Delilah went from looking alarmed to looking dumbfounded. Jack was beginning to question his judgment in putting Philo on the team.

"O-okay . . . ," said Delilah. "I better get these guys working on their masterpiece. But first"—she touched Jack's shoulder and leaned in close—"can I have a word? I just remembered something."

Todd and Brett started packing up their equipment, leaving Darylyn, Philo, and Reese standing around looking slightly lost. Jack let himself be led away by Delilah.

"What is it?" he asked.

Delilah crossed her arms. "This girlfriend of yours, the one you mentioned the first day of filming. Nats. We haven't seen her. We haven't got any footage of her. She should really be with you when you open the balloon festival."

"Oh," said Jack. "Um. Well—"

"Be straight with me, Jack. She doesn't exist, does she?"

"Of course she exists!" said Jack.

This, at least, was technically true. Nats *did* exist. Just not in a being-the-girlfriend-of-Jack-Sprigley sense.

Delilah stared at him for a moment. "I'm not judging you.

I just want to know: Is this is another thing I need to 'make happen'? Because I'm going to be extremely busy between now and the weekend, getting the plans for these two balloons to the seamstresses—"

"*Two* balloons?"

Delilah looked temporarily lost for words. "It's just . . . insurance. In case the first one doesn't work out." She looked Jack in the eye. "So we're solid on the Nats thing? There's nothing I need to do?"

Jack wondered if Delilah really *could* find a way to fix him up with Nats. She'd already proved she had the power to change reality. Jack snapped his fingers, Delilah transported him to a firing range, summoned up a fishing boat, pulled the strings to make him Mayor for a Week. It just fell into his lap, without him even having to do anything. He was starting to wonder if that was a good thing.

"No," he said. "It's all good. It's all taken care of."

From the way Delilah was looking at him, Jack got the feeling she didn't totally buy it.

"Okay," she said reluctantly. "I just don't want any nasty surprises on the night."

"There won't be any surprises," promised Jack.

He glanced across the room at Vivi.

There'd been enough of those already.

Chapter Twenty-Two

~~~~~~

And this," said Mayor Perry-Moore, "is my office."

Jack and Vivi stood in the carpeted hallway outside the mayor's chambers. Jack had taken off the mayoral robes as soon as the swearing-in ceremony was over. They were now being carried by the woman from the council who'd spoken at the school, as the mayor gave Jack and Vivi a tour of the council offices where they'd be spending most of the next week.

As far as Jack knew, Delilah was off filming Darylyn and Philo and Reese in the computer lab at school, where they were busy designing Jack's balloon for the festival. He hoped she was going to be back to get plenty of footage of him in junior mayor mode. The producers needed to see him looking powerful and important if he was going to stand a chance of being voted onto the Bigwigs Board.

Mayor Perry-Moore was about to show Jack and Vivi through to his office when one of his phones buzzed. It was the third text in as many minutes. And just like the other times, it wasn't the slim BlackBerry in his left jacket pocket that was buzzing; it was the cheap, basic-looking phone he kept in the other pocket.

"Sorry," he said, a smirk playing at the corners of his mouth as he read the text. "Just got to answer this."

With that, the mayor disappeared into his office, the door swinging not-quite-closed behind him.

"He might be in there a while," said the woman from the council. "Can I get anything for either of you? A glass of water?"

Jack shook his head. Vivi asked for a mineral water. "Apple and guava would be great."

"I'm not sure we—"

"Hmmm," said Vivi, frowning with junior deputy mayoral disappointment.

The woman smiled a tight smile. "I'll see what I can do."

Once the woman was gone, Vivi turned on Jack and stood there glaring at him, arms crossed over her chest. "I didn't say this before, because I didn't want to embarrass you in front of everyone. But now we're alone, I'm going to call you out for the selfish, self-serving backstabber that you are."

Jack raised his eyebrows. "Okay, that's kind of harsh. . . ."

"It's not harsh at all. I was about to do something really cool with this Mayor for a Week thing, and you stole it from me." She glanced toward the half-shut door to the mayor's office, then leaned over to Jack. "You don't even deserve it," she hissed. "You just got it because you cheated."

"First of all," said Jack, lowering his voice, "Mayor for a Week is not even *that* cool."

"True," conceded Vivi. "But it was *my* not-that-cool thing."

"Second," Jack continued, undeterred, "you can't say I *stole* it. It's not like you knew for sure you were going to get it."

"You're right, Jack. It's really unlikely I was going to win. I mean, they only went and made me deputy when they couldn't make me mayor. Upland doesn't even have an *actual* deputy mayor. Think about *that* for a second—I'm a junior version of something that doesn't even exist!"

"Sure, and you're the only person in the world who's ever had to put up with being in second place," Jack muttered.

Vivi frowned. "What's that supposed to mean?"

Jack ignored the question. "And you're wrong about me not deserving it, anyway. I was on *Bigwigs*, remember? I've done this kind of thing before. That's *real-world* experience, right there."

"Reality TV is *not* the real world, Jack."

"It's more real than writing an essay," he snapped back. "And while we're on the topic of betrayals, let's talk about you and Reese and Darylyn, shall we? I spent the whole break not knowing if we were even *friends* or not. You guys *ditched* me. I get that Reese and Darylyn were probably busy 'getting to know each other'—and, yes, I mean that in a totally disgusting way. And now it's pretty obvious that you and Sampson were doing the same thing." He swayed his pelvis in a vague attempt to simulate whatever it was he imagined Vivi and Sampson had been doing all break. Which, judging by his impression, was a cross between practicing the samba and playing the party game of passing oranges to one another with their knees.

Vivi looked disturbed. "That wasn't . . . You've got it *totally* wrong. I'd barely spoken a *word* to Oliver before that soccer match."

"Well, you've definitely been making up for lost time."

"Now you're just being gross. But, actually, you're right. I *have* gotten to know him since then. And I think you're being totally unfair to him."

Jack wondered how well Vivi *really* knew Sampson. Did she know he'd called Jack a "baldy-balls" in front of everyone else in the locker room? Did she know about his secret identity as ModLSkillz, bad-mouthing Jack on the *Bigwigs* forum?

"There's something you don't know about Oliver," said

Vivi, stealing the very same words that Jack was gearing up to say. "I shouldn't be telling you this, but Oliver sent in an application for *Bigwigs,* the year after you were on. And they said no. He lost to someone else. Which, I don't know, might sound familiar? I'm just saying."

"Right," said Jack, rolling his eyes. "And that makes me the all-around worst person ever."

"*Bigwigs* is like a beehive of bad memories for Oliver," Vivi went on. "And now you're poking and prodding at it with this reunion episode thing. You've probably undone *months* of therapy."

That was sort of the idea, thought Jack. He'd had to fight back against Sampson's testosterone firestorm somehow. It wasn't *his* fault that *Bigwigs* was the only weapon he had.

"Yeah," he said sarcastically. "Poor Sampson, with all his freakishly enormous man-parts. I bet *that* sucks." He crooked his elbow into his groin and let his arm dangle forward like an elephant's trunk, then swayed it from side to side as he honked out the words, "What. A. Tragedy."

"Here's your mineral water, Miss Junior Deputy Mayor."

Jack looked awkwardly over his shoulder as the woman returned and handed Vivi a bottle of pale-green mineral water with a straw in it. He couldn't think of any way to explain what he was doing, so he just held his pose.

"I won't ask," said the woman.

"I'd struggle for an answer, to be honest," said Jack, straightening up again.

The woman looked into the mayor's office and said, "I think he's ready for you."

Vivi leaned toward Jack as they were both ushered inside. "I don't know what your deal is with Oliver," she whispered. "But if you could give him a job on your team—if you gave him some proper screen time on *Bigwigs*—then I might not think you're a totally awful person." She pulled out her phone. "I'm texting you his number now. So you've got no excuse."

Jack had no intention of giving Sampson any more *Bigwigs* screen time. "What if he says no?"

"Then I'll just assume you weren't trying hard enough. Either that, or . . ."

"Or what?"

"Or that you really don't care what I think of you."

Jack couldn't believe it. The reason all of this had happened in the *first* place was because he cared what Vivi and Reese and Darylyn thought of him. He was so concerned about their opinion of him that he'd tried to fake puberty to stay friends with them.

Did he really have it in him to keep up that charade and be a Good Samaritan to Sampson as well?

Chapter Twenty-Three

~~~~~~

Jack spent his second day as Mayor for a Week getting in and out of the council limousine and posing for photo opportunities with magistrates, the police chief, fire wardens, and other important townsfolk.

Todd and Brett trailed him the whole time in their mini-van, filming the photo ops and small talk. Jack figured Delilah was busy making sure she had everything in place to bring his reunion show clip package to a suitably impressive climax.

His big ballooning moment was only days away. Soon he'd be standing up in front of the whole town to launch the balloon festival, before soaring through the heavens to victory in his very own mayoral chariot.

With his official duties finally over for the day, Jack grabbed himself an energy shake and walked home via the Ninth Street Mall. All through the day, everywhere he'd gone, he'd been welcomed like a king. Every door in Upland was open to him.

It was almost enough to stop him thinking about the typically disappointing results of that morning's pube tally. (Zero.)

And it was almost enough to stop him thinking about the guilt trip Vivi had laid on him the day before.

Upland's newly sworn-in Deputy Mayor for a Week had been sitting in on council subcommittee meetings all day. But Jack figured that was probably Vivi's idea of fun. She would've hated being driven all around town and having to meet and greet the townsfolk, he decided. If anything, he'd done her *a favor* by making her deputy.

He thought about calling Sampson, like Vivi had asked him to. He'd been putting it off. He didn't want Sampson soaking up his precious time on camera. And he definitely didn't want Sampson standing in the same frame as him, making him look small when he needed more than ever to look big.

The producers must have had a good reason for rejecting Sampson from *Bigwigs* in the first place. Jack didn't see why it was suddenly *his* responsibility to give Sampson *Bigwigs* screen time.

Especially not now, when Jack still had to convince everyone he was Bigwigs Board material.

Jack's phone rang. For a moment he was worried it was Vivi, calling to guilt him, but it was Darylyn.

"Hey," he answered. "Is the balloon ready?"

"It's done," said Darylyn, sounding slightly offended at Jack's presumption of anything less than 100 percent efficiency on her part. "I've got the 3-D file right here on my laptop. But—"

"But what?"

"The design Philo's come up with. It has what I would call a significant emphasis on dried fruits."

"Oh yeah, that's okay," said Jack. "That was the plan."

It turned out Philo *hadn't* gotten the morning off from the Raisin World stand to help Jack move into his bachelor pad. He'd skipped his shift, and he was in his parents' bad books, big-time. Jack figured that turning the hot-air balloon into a free advertisement for Raisin World might help Philo balance the ledger.

"Just confirming you're okay with it being so . . . raisin-focused," said Darylyn.

As long as it's not covered in pubes, thought Jack. He was about to ask Darylyn to send him through a screenshot of the 3-D file, just to be sure, when he spotted a lone figure doing some window shopping farther down the mall, causing him to lose his train of thought.

Former Mayor for a Week and Jack's-girlfriend-who-didn't-know-it-yet: Natsumi Distagio.

"It's all good," Jack replied vaguely. "Gotta go." He hit end call and picked up his mayoral stride again. "That's right," he barked, pretending to speak into the phone. "You tell those pen pushers at town hall to pull out all the stops. This balloon festival's too damn important to wrap up in red tape. I don't want to hear any more 'No we can't.' I want to hear 'Yes we can!' You got that?"

Nats spun around. She clutched the straps of her sequined slouch bag with one hand, and half a dozen shopping bags with the other. Jack pretended not to see her at first. Then she leaned to one side and waved at him, shopping bags dangling from her arm.

"Oh, h-hey, Natsumi," he said, aiming for laid-back, but not quite managing to keep the tremor from his voice.

"Jack! Who were you talking to just now?" Nats made a show of looking concerned. "It sounded serious!"

Jack rolled his eyes. "Just some official Mayor for a Week business. This phone will *not* stop ringing. I mean, I'm not telling you anything you don't know. You've been there. You know what it's like, being the big man in town."

Nats blushed.

"Big woman!" Jack corrected himself. "You would have been more of a big woman. I mean, you still are, obviously. A big, big woman."

He sucked nervously on the straw of his energy shake

while Nats stared awkwardly down at her feet.

"Anyway," said Jack, quickly moving on. "My point is that being Mayor for a Week is cuh-razy."

Nats nodded. "It's so rewarding, but it's a *lot* of pressure."

"Totally," said Jack. "And on top of the usual craziness, there's the hot-air balloon festival happening on the weekend. I'm even racing in my own special Mayor for a Week balloon. I'm calling it Hot-Air Force One."

"Nice!" Nats snorted with laughter. Jack felt his confidence creep up a notch.

"And, you know, I've also got this film crew following me around the whole time. . . ."

"That's right!" said Nats, taking Jack's bait, just as he'd hoped. "The *Bigwigs* thing! It's weird, Hals keeps giving me the brush-off whenever I ask about it. I'm like, how can you be so meh about it? It's *TV*!"

"It is. It *is* TV." Jack swallowed nervously. "And speaking of TV . . . I mean, if you ever wanted to get in front of the cameras . . . you know, before they wrap up the shoot . . ."

Nats looked at him expectantly.

"I'm just saying, it wouldn't be hard to arrange."

"Really?"

Jack stroked his chin thoughtfully. "The only thing is, we'd need to come up with a good reason why we'd be hanging out together. . . ."

"Well, I'm friends with your sister, so . . . ?"

Jack screwed up his face. "Yeah, but Hallie's doing her best to avoid being on camera. I don't know, I kind of get the feeling she'd bring down the vibe and spoil your big moment."

Nats shrugged. "Well, we could just pretend we know each other some other way?"

"Interesting," said Jack, nodding meditatively. "What . . . sort of thing did you have in mind?"

A "eureka" look flashed across Nats's face. "I've got it! The Mayor for a Week program! I could be your mentor. That way I get to show everyone my serious and intelligent side."

"Hmm," said Jack, doing his best to look as though he was giving it serious consideration. "Interesting idea. I'm just wondering . . . What if, *instead* of that, we tweaked the setup a little—just a tiny bit—and you, I don't know . . ."

Jack took a deep breath and went for it.

". . . *pretendedtobemygirlfriend.*"

~~~~~~

Chapter Twenty-Four

Nats blinked. "Did you just say I should pretend to be your *girlfriend?*"

"My hot older girlfriend." Jack shrugged, as though he'd suggested nothing more controversial than ordering a side of garlic bread with dinner. "Just an idea."

Nats's face soured into a look of distaste. "I don't think so, Jack."

"You're right," he sighed. "*Bigwigs* is going prime time this season, there's going to be so many people watching it, all across the country. . . . I guess it'd be hard to make *all those viewers* believe we're really a couple. You'd need to be, like, a really awesome actress to pull *that* off." Jack could see Nats processing what he'd just said. He waited a moment before playing his winning card. "It'd be like . . . what do they call it when you do an audition in front of a camera?"

The sourness seemed to fade slightly. "A screen test?"

"That's it. It'd be like doing a really big, important screen test."

Nats hooked her thumb inside her necklace and ran it up and down the length of the chain as she pondered. "Well, when you put it like that . . . I guess if I thought of it like an acting job . . ."

Jack nodded encouragingly.

"And I *am* between boyfriends . . . ," Nats went on.

"Does that mean you'll do it?" His voice rose up on the words "do it" and wavered out of control for a second, like he'd swallowed a theremin. He put it down to nerves.

Luckily, Nats didn't seem to have noticed. She narrowed her eyes. "How girlfriend-y do I have to be?"

Jack tried to look nonchalant. He made sure to pitch his voice low, to keep those nerves from making themselves heard again. "Just . . . you know. The usual stuff."

"Like what?"

Jack realized he had no idea. He pictured a pair of "His" and "Hers" bath towels, for some reason. "I don't know. . . . Just enough to make it look convincing for the cameras, I guess."

Nats seemed to steel herself. She glanced up and down the mall, then dragged an unresisting Jack around the corner into an arcade. When she seemed sure no one was looking, she put her bags down on the ground and draped a slender arm over his narrow shoulders.

Holy crap, thought Jack.

Nats turned to face an invisible, imaginary camera in the distance somewhere.

"This is Jack," she said brightly, pulling him closer. "He's my boyfriend. We've been together for . . . how long now?"

Jack became a fountain of sweat. "Um . . . a month?" His face was fully smooshed against her now. Through the thin layer of her cotton jersey he felt the underwire from her right bra cup dig into his cheek. Not even the realization that something as exciting and mysterious as a bra was held together by something as boring and unsexy as wire could keep his pulse from racing.

"Let's make it two," whispered Nats. She turned back to the imaginary camera. "Two whole months we've been together!" With her free hand, she patted Jack gently on the head.

Jack glanced up apologetically. "Um, maybe don't do the head-patting thing when we're on camera for real?"

"Sorry." Nats closed her eyes and went very zen for a moment, as though collecting herself for a Shakespeare debut.

With the hand she'd used to pat Jack on the head, she grabbed Jack's left hand and placed it around her waist. His hand came to rest on her left hip.

Jack's instinct was to lift his hand away and run. Just run. Instead, he kept it frozen where it was, not moving a muscle, worried a sudden spasm might cause him to accidentally goose Nats and break the spell.

Nats shook her head in response to an imaginary question. "No, the age gap isn't a problem. Jack's very mature. He's not like other boys his age. Most seventh-grade boys—"

"Um, eighth-grade?"

Nats blinked. "Most eighth-grade boys would be too embarrassed to be in a relationship like this. They wouldn't know what to do, or wouldn't respect certain boundaries."

"I . . . definitely respect your boundaries," said Jack. He looked up at Nats, wondering if she was likely to notice the damp, sweaty handprint he was almost certainly leaving on her leggings.

"That's why we're so good together," she finished.

Wow, thought Jack. Nats was really getting into character. Maybe she *did* have talent as a performer. And maybe, just maybe, this whole "older girlfriend" ploy had a chance of succeeding. Maybe he was going to be able to keep up with the Amit Gondras of the world after all.

"You're a really good actress," said Jack.

Nats shrugged. She picked up her bags from where she'd left them on the ground.

"Or . . . maybe there really *is* something between us?" Jack gulped.

Nats locked eyes with him.

"No. I was acting." She glanced down at her shopping bags and then looked up at Jack again. "People like me? We're always acting."

Jack frowned. What did she mean by that? And people like *what*? Popular people who everyone wanted to be friends with, and who had everything they wanted?

"So it's a deal then? You'll come up onstage with me at the festival? You'll pretend to be my girlfriend for the cameras?"

Nats passed her phone to Jack. "We should swap numbers. So I know where to be on the night."

That sounds like a yes, thought Jack. He handed Nats his phone, hoping she wouldn't notice the sweaty residue he'd left on it.

They entered their numbers and passed the phones back to each other. Jack still couldn't quite believe what had happened. He now had a little part of Nats to carry around with him, and Nats had a little part of Jack to carry around with her, too.

At least until after the balloon festival, when Jack was

99 percent sure she'd delete his number and never speak to him again.

Or maybe the TV cameras would show just how well matched they were, and they'd become a celebrity power couple for real and forever.

Nats slipped her phone back into her bag. "Bye, Jack. Enjoy the rest of your time at the top." She smiled weakly. "I'll see you over the weekend."

"Y-yeah," said Jack, his grip tightening around his phone out of fear of it slipping from his hands. "See you then. B-babe."

"What?"

Jack shook his head. "Nothing." He stood and watched his newly minted fake girlfriend walk off into the distance. As soon as she was out of sight, he jabbed at his phone, making sure her number really was in there.

It was. It really was. She'd even put a smiley after her name.

A. Smiley.

It was almost enough to make him forget about the other new entry in his list of recently added contacts. But there it was, directly under Nats.

Oliver Sampson.

Jack stared at the name. He was starting to realize he'd been carrying a little part of *Sampson* around with him for way too long. The part that made Jack feel like the smallest kid in school. Now he was the biggest man in town—and he actually felt like it. Not only that, but he had his own bachelor pad, and his very own mega-hottie to go with it. *Bigwigs* was sure to want him back. He was a completely different person now. Jack Sprigley: bigger and better. It almost didn't matter that he didn't have pubes yet. Everything else had fallen into place.

He'd faked the big time.

Flushed with these strange new feelings of conquest and triumph, Jack hit dial.

Sampson sounded confused when he answered. "Um, yeah? Who's this?"

Jack cleared his throat. "It's Jack. Jack Sprigley."

There was a pause. "What do *you* want? Aren't you busy being Upland's Incredibly Junior Mayor?"

Jack ignored Sampson's jibe. He wanted to strike the right balance between victorious and generous. *Magnanimous,* he thought. That was the word he was after. Like a tennis champion shaking hands with a crushed and broken rival. "I just wanted to see if you were coming to the balloon festival on Friday night. It's the last bit of filming before I fly down for the live show, and—"

"And you just wanted to remind me how great you are?"

"No, I just thought you might want to be part of it. The

whole *Bigwigs* thing. You know, get yourself on camera a bit more—"

"So, basically hang around in the background like a Jack Sprigley fanboy?"

"It doesn't have to be that. You could help unveil this balloon I'm racing in—"

"Nah, thanks." Sampson's tone changed completely. He sounded weirdly casual. Almost friendly—but with an undertone that Jack couldn't quite figure out. "I'm good."

Jack didn't want Vivi thinking he hadn't tried hard enough. "I just thought, since everyone else is going to be at the festival, you might as well be there too. Part of the gang." He hoped Vivi appreciated how much it pained him to say that.

"Oh, don't worry," said Sampson. "I'll definitely be there." He paused, and the silence on the other end of the line was as bad as any embarrassing locker room put-down. "Catch you later, Sprogless."

Jack's phone beeped three times.

Call ended.

Chapter Twenty-Five

~~~~~~

Delilah unclipped her seat belt and leaned across to Jack. "Here we are, Mr. Mayor for a Week. Your big moment."

They'd pulled up in the VIP area behind the grandstand at the Upland Showgrounds. Jack, Delilah, Todd, and Brett piled out of the minivan. On the other side of the grandstand, the Fourteenth Annual Upland Hot-Air Balloon Festival was bobbing into action. Food stalls and sideshows ringed the edge of the Number One Oval. Hundreds of people milled about, and more were arriving every minute. In the center of the oval, Jack counted twenty or thirty hot-air balloons floating ten feet above the grass, tethered to the ground by thick white ropes. Festivalgoers took rides in the baskets, posing for selfies or waving to their friends and families below. Occasionally a jet of flame lit up a balloon from within, accompanied by a roar like that of a caged animal straining to be set loose.

Over on the Number Two Oval, festival staff in fluorescent vests checked wind direction and communicated with one another via walkie-talkie as they cordoned off an area for the Mayor's Balloon Race. Jack had discovered it was more of a timed flight than an actual race. The challenging team—chosen by lottery, and this year flying in a balloon sponsored by Avocado World—would make a short flight from one side of the oval to the other, where they had to land as close as possible to a painted X on the grass. The mayor's team, also chosen by lottery, had to make the same flight and beat the time the challenger had set.

"Okay," said Delilah. "We're going to go and film some local color. We'll meet you back here in half an hour. The limousine should have arrived by then. Then we'll get you into your robes and chains and film your big entrance." Delilah looked Jack in the eye. "With Natsumi."

"With Natsumi," said Jack. He should have been sounding confident. It was all figured out. And he'd done it on his own. He'd made Nats his pretend girlfriend all by himself. But it wasn't Nats he was worried about.

Jack watched Delilah and her crew head through one of the gates and out into the festival, then scanned the oval for any sign of Oliver Sampson. He'd said he was coming. He'd said he was definitely going to be there.

And he'd sounded like he was up to something.

"*Someone's* looking jittery," said a voice behind him.

Jack turned to see Vivi standing there, armed with an access pass and a clipboard. She was supposed to spend the opening night stationed at the main tent, helping Jack get organized for his speech. It was the only job anyone had been able to think to give her. Jack saw the woman from the council stationed at the organizers' tent as well, keeping an eye on things.

"You're not *nervous*, are you?" said Vivi. "Didn't you tell me you've done this kind of thing before? Isn't that why you're so much more qualified to be Mayor for a Week than I am?"

Jack wasn't nervous about his launch speech. Public speaking had never bothered him, he knew where he had to be, and he'd memorized his script. He'd make his grand entrance (arm in arm with Nats, if everything went to plan), then get up on the grandstand to declare the festival open (again, ideally arm in arm with Nats), then pose for the news cameras and *Bigwigs* camera as his hot-air balloon design for the Mayor's Balloon Race was unveiled.

But that didn't mean he wasn't nervous. He'd woken up with faint red spots—some sort of weird stress rash, he guessed—creeping up his neck. "Have you seen Sampson?" he asked.

Vivi looked him in the eye. "No. I haven't."

"I called him," Jack insisted. "I spoke to him."

"And?"

And ever since then I've had a very bad feeling about this whole thing, thought Jack.

Jack's phone buzzed before he could describe his conversation with Sampson to Vivi. Vivi peered over his shoulder as he checked the message. "Oliver?" she asked.

Jack said nothing. Instead, he looked up from his phone and scanned the area near the gate. There she was, in an expensive-looking black dress and gold jewelry. The crowning detail in Jack's plan to out-Bigwig the other Bigwigs.

Natsumi saw Jack and waved. Jack couldn't help noticing the dark look on Vivi's face. "I'm giving Nats her big break," he explained with a shrug.

"And you get a trophy wife for the cameras." Vivi clasped her hands to her chest. "Or—wait, could it be true love? A love that transcends grade levels! A love that transcends her being a ditz and you being—"

"Me being what?"

Vivi unclasped her hands and scowled, but didn't answer.

She focused intently on her clipboard for a moment.

Jack went over to meet Nats at the gate, waving his access pass at the security guards so they'd let her through. When Jack realized that Vivi had followed him over, he instinctively reached out toward Nats as if to put his arm around her.

Nats shrank away slightly. "Um, only for the cameras, remember?"

"Yeah, right. I get it. I was just . . . practicing."

"Ugh," said Vivi.

"Speaking of cameras, I guess we should go and find Delilah." Jack leaned closer to Nats. "She's my producer."

"She's the *Bigwigs* segment producer," Vivi corrected him.

Jack ignored her. "They're going to film us arriving together in a limousine."

Nats looked confused. "But we're already here!"

"They're going to fake it," said Vivi, putting on a sarcastically sympathetic smile. "Like everything Jack does."

"That's how it works in TV." Jack held his hands out in a "what can you do about it?" gesture. "That's showbiz, babe."

Vivi looked unwell. "You did not just call her 'babe.'"

In the nick of time, Jack spotted Darylyn, Philo, and Reese heading across the oval toward them. "Hey, there's my team!" He waved them over, then turned to Nats. "Before we find Delilah, let's see if we can go and check out Hot-Air

Force One. I've been wanting to see this all week!"

"That's Natsumi Distagio," Darylyn observed, as she and Reese and Philo arrived at the gate where Jack and the others were.

"Correct," said Vivi.

"Can we see the balloon?" asked Jack.

Darylyn nodded, with an ever-so-slightly concerned look on her face. "They're doing a test inflation now."

Reese threw Jack a look. "It's not the only thing that's getting inflated around here." He nodded toward Vivi. "Hey, dude, how's Mayor for a Week treating you?"

"Reese, you know I'm deputy."

"I know who *should* have been mayor."

Darylyn glanced at Reese, then Vivi, then Jack. "I suggest we go look at the balloon."

Darylyn and Reese led the way through the gate and past the organizers' tent, with Vivi and Nats making an awkward second pairing. A crew in fluorescent vests was busy laying out a nylon envelope on the grass. A wicker basket lay on its side nearby.

Philo hung back and gave Jack a nudge. "So I never asked: Did you find that stuff I left for you?"

Jack frowned. "What stuff?"

"The stuff!"

Jack shook his head, frowning. "But I asked you about it,

remember? You said you didn't leave anything in the bachelor pad."

"I didn't leave anything in the bachelor pad."

"Okay. So . . ."

"I left it in your room."

Jack stopped. "Wait, what? The bachelor pad *is* my
room."

"Is it?"

"I swapped rooms with my gran. You helped me move
my things!"

"Oh. Right." Philo paused. "So I guess that means I left
it in your *old* room."

"My *old* room? But that's . . ." Jack stopped and grabbed
Philo by the shoulders. "Okay, Philo, listen to me carefully.
This is important. *What* did you *leave* in my *gran's room?*"

Philo looked thoughtful. "Maybe it doesn't work on
ladies."

"Philo!"

"Okeydoke. So you know how people always seem to do
what my family tells them to do? Well, I went to the doctor
and made him give me this cream I found out about. Except
here's the brilliant part. It's not for me. It's for *you*."

"Cream? What sort of cream?"

"It's a . . . wait a minute, I always have trouble with this . . .
It's a tes-toster-own cream."

Jack's eyes widened. "A *what*?"

"It makes your pubes grow! Anyway, I put it right on that little table next to your bed."

"*Gran's* bed! *Gran's* little table!"

Philo paused. "I did wonder why you had a photo of yourself there."

Jack tried to calm down. Maybe Marlene hadn't seen it. She kept all sorts of junk on her bedside table. It was possible that Philo's well-meaning but wildly misdirected gift had gone unnoticed. "Okay. Let's think for a moment. What else was on the table?"

"Well, it's funny you should say that, because there were a whole bunch of other creams there too."

Oh God, thought Jack. *Other creams. Moisturizers. Cleansers. Face creams.*

"I think it'll be fine," said Philo, noticing Jack's panicked expression. "I mean, your gran is very old and probably has a lot of pubes already, so she might not even notice."

Jack did his best to ignore the mental image Philo had just conjured. "It's *testosterone* cream, Philo. It has to do more than just *give you pubes*. I mean, are there any side effects?"

Before Philo could answer, Jack heard someone shout his name from across the showgrounds. Hallie was tearing toward him with the Shieling twins in tow. The security guards at the gate didn't even stop them to check for access passes, so intense was the look on Hallie's face. At first Jack was worried she was about to yell at him for stealing Nats away from her—but then he realized she looked more freaked out than furious.

"What's wrong? What are you doing here?"

Yasmine crossed her arms over her chest. "*We're* here because we wanted to see Natsumi make a spectacle of herself."

Hallie didn't seem to be relishing Nats's fall from grace the way the Shieling twins were. "Jack, I got a call from Mom. It's Gran. Something weird's happened."

Jack glanced sideways at Philo. "Yeah, I think—"

"Jack, she's in the hospital."

There were gasps. Nats clamped her hand to her mouth.

Jack blinked. "What? What happened?"

"Okay, this is the weird part. Mom thinks she attacked a taxi driver."

"*What?*"

"Like, actually pinned him down and nearly broke his arm."

"Wait, so it's the *taxi driver* who got injured?"

"Both," said Hallie. "Mom says Gran slipped and cut her head open. She's okay, but there's cops at the hospital. She's worried the taxi driver's going to press charges."

"Against *Gran*?" Jack gave a nervous laugh. "Nah, Mom

must be pranking you." He checked his phone. "Look, no messages."

"Yeah, I guess she figured you were too busy to bother with boring family stuff *like your gran committing assault.*" Hallie closed her eyes and took a deep breath. "But let's forget about that. I don't care about that *Bigwigs* stuff anymore. This is more important. Remember Gran going all *Exorcist* the other night? I think she might have stopped taking her hormone pills."

"What hormone pills?"

Hallie rolled her eyes. "The ones you pick up for her every month?"

"They're *hormone pills*?" Jack's brow crinkled. "I've been buying *lady hormone pills*?"

"It's not just pills," said Philo. "You can get creams as well. Like the tes-toster-own cream I bought for Jack and accidentally left in his gran's room."

Everyone turned and stared at Philo.

Hallie blinked. "Did he just say he gave *testosterone cream* to Gran?"

Jack put a hand to his brow and groaned. Surely this wasn't happening. Not now. Not when his audition for the Bigwigs Board was at stake.

"You know what?" said Hallie. "It doesn't even matter at this point. Jack, we've got to go to the hospital. Mom's probably stressed out of her head."

"Yeah, but—" Jack glanced at Nats, and gestured at the bobbing sea of hot-air balloons above the oval. "There's all *this*. . . ."

Nats stared at Jack in disbelief. "Jack! This is your *family* we're talking about!"

Jack clutched his access pass. "But . . . this is a big deal—"

Nats stepped away from him, looking disgusted. "Hals, I'll drive you to the hospital."

With a final glare over her shoulder at Jack, Nats pulled Hallie after her through the gate toward the parking lot. The Shieling twins took the opportunity to melt back into the crowd, but not without shooting Jack identical dirty looks first.

Jack couldn't believe it. His *fake* girlfriend had *actually* dumped him.

He realized everybody was staring at him. "What?" he said. "It's tough, okay? It's not easy, balancing work and family." He scratched at his neck as his stress rash started to itch. "But I'm Mayor for a Week. I've got responsibilities. I'm the man of the house, but I'm also the big man in town." He pointed over to where the crew had started inflating his race balloon. "Someone's got to fly in Hot-Air Force One."

The basket was on its side, tethered to the ground, and the crew was using a large fan to blow air into the nylon balloon.

Slowly the balloon that Philo had designed and Darylyn had modeled took shape before Jack's eyes. The balloon seemed to be made up of two segments—two bumpy ovoid shapes—joined together in the middle. The fabric was decorated all over with folds and furrows that made the balloon look puckered and shriveled.

Jack realized it was supposed to look like a pair of raisins. What it actually looked like was—

"A scrotum," he said out loud. "Hot-Air Force One looks like a massive scrotum."

Philo tilted his head to one side. "Now that you mention it . . ."

The crew lit the gas burner and the scrotum-shaped balloon began a majestic rise into the air. Jack saw the crew stand back to look at it, appraising it properly for the first time. They frowned and rubbed their chins. One of them nudged another. There was chuckling and shaking of heads. A couple of them turned and looked right at Jack.

Jack rounded on Philo and Darylyn. "What the hell? What the *hell*? How am I supposed to fly in *that*?"

Darylyn shrugged. "I did try to tell you."

"You told me it had a bit of a 'dried fruit' vibe. You didn't tell me it looked like a giant pair of *baldy-balls*!" Jack turned to Reese. "What about you? You were there. You saw them work on this."

Reese shrugged. "Dude, if I'd said something, would it have made a difference? You're so wrapped up in your own head all the time. The only reason it took me so long to tell you about me and D was because I knew you'd freak out and start thinking you didn't 'measure up' or something. Everything's a *competition* with you. Dude, I'm over it."

Before Jack could answer, Philo pointed into the distance and said, "We probably should have gone with a design more like *that*." Farther afield in the area behind the grandstand, blotting out the setting sun and lit up by great bursts of flame, was a fiery red balloon shaped like a rocket. Its flanks were emblazoned with the Avocado World logo.

Standing at the base of the balloon, gathered around the basket, was a fluorescent-vested crew much like the one that was preparing Jack's balloon. But this balloon was not generating chuckles among the crew. This balloon demanded solemn, masculine respect. The *Bigwigs* crew was there too, Jack suddenly noticed. And Delilah was right there with them, interviewing someone.

Interviewing Oliver Sampson.

Two balloons, thought Jack. Back at the swearing-in for Mayor for a Week, Delilah had said she needed to arrange for two balloons. And now he realized: One of those balloons was for Oliver Sampson.

Just like she'd rigged the selection of Mayor for a Week

in Jack's favor, Delilah must have rigged the lottery so that Sampson would be flying against Jack. She was *finding the story.* Suddenly Jack realized what that was going to be. His "story" on the *Bigwigs* reunion special was going to end in a dramatic race between Sampson's penis-rocket and Jack's tragic testicles. Jack's audition for the Bigwigs Board was going to be a massive joke—with Sampson laughing hardest.

It was over, Jack realized. The more he'd tried to fake the big time, the smaller he'd become.

He took off his access pass and dropped it on the ground. "I'm out," he said. He turned and walked toward the gate.

"Jack!" Vivi called after him.

But Jack didn't answer. He didn't stop, or turn around.

Instead, he ran.

Part Three

Bring Back Jack

Chapter Twenty-Six

The shuttle bus from the showgrounds pulled up at the Ninth Street Mall. Jack was the only passenger. Everyone else was heading toward the festival, not away from it.

Jack squeezed his way out through the front door as passengers bound for the festival piled on board. None of them seemed to recognize him, or wonder why the Mayor for a Week was leaving the festival when he was meant to be launching it. As far as they knew, the kid leaving the bus was just that: a kid.

The shuttle bus pulled away, and the mall was left dark and empty. Jack cut a dazed path past the shop fronts, wandering from one end of the mall to the other. All the doors that had seemed open to him just a few days ago were closed.

Jack crouched in the arcade where he and Nats had rehearsed being girlfriend and boyfriend. He rested his head in his hands.

And he sat there for a long, long time.

Nobody had come after him. He wasn't surprised. Vivi and Reese and Darylyn had been desperate to ditch him since before the start of second semester. Nothing he'd done since then had changed that. If anything, he'd made things worse. First by *still* not growing pubes, and then by everything else he'd done.

He'd half expected Delilah to send her cameras after him, though, to capture a dramatic grab for the reunion show. He imagined her pitching the scene. *("'See how far a Bigwig can fall.' It'll be great TV.")* But she'd obviously decided that Sampson deserved the spotlight more than Jack.

Nats had abandoned him too. Only a couple of days ago she'd put her number in his phone. Who knew where things might have gone from there? But as it turned out, they'd gone nowhere.

Typical for some family crisis to screw things up. Jack felt a twinge of guilt about his gran, but he pushed it aside. It was all Philo's fault, anyway. It wasn't like Jack had *asked* for the testosterone cream that had turned Marlene into Granzilla.

Jack sighed and took out his phone. No messages.

With a feeling of grim satisfaction, he went into his contacts and deleted Nats's number—smiley and all.

The next number in the list was Oliver Sampson's. Jack felt a flash of hot anger. He wished he could delete Sampson from more than just his phone.

His finger hovered above Sampson's name, ready to swipe him into oblivion, when a call came through.

Jack stared at the screen in disbelief as the phone kept ringing and buzzing in his hand. The name that had come up as the caller was the very same one he had been poised to delete.

What was Oliver Sampson doing calling him? Only Jack's prepubescent lack of physical strength kept him from crushing the phone in his hand.

How? he thought. How did Sampson *always* manage to appear just at the right moment to make things worse? First he'd stolen Jack's friends, then he'd stolen *Bigwigs*. What was he hoping to take from Jack now?

Maybe he was just angry and wanting to give Jack a piece of his mind. Jack had denied Sampson the chance to completely humiliate him in the balloon race. He'd ruined Sampson's big moment in front of the *Bigwigs* cameras.

Jack hit ignore call and then deleted Sampson from his contacts.

Another call. This time, the caller came up as just a number, with no name attached.

Jack hit ignore again.

Another call.

Jack was genuinely tempted to throw the phone away. He didn't need it. Nobody was ever going to call him again anyway. He hit ignore.

Again, like a jab in the arm, the phone rang. Jack hit answer and unleashed his pent-up rage into the phone. "*What?* What do you want? Why won't you leave me alone?"

"Sprigley?"

Jack felt the heat rise off him into the night air. "Oh, it's 'Sprigley' now, is it? Not 'Sprogless.' Not 'baldy-balls.'"

"Jack?" Sampson's voice sounded low and quiet. It sounded small.

"Yes! Of course it's me! What do you even want? Shouldn't you be breaking records in your wiener-zeppelin by now?"

"I'm not at the festival," whispered Sampson. "I left."

Jack presumed it wasn't out of solidarity, or flattery by imitation. Still, he was mildly curious. "You left?"

"I got your address out of that Dawson weirdo and I took a taxi straight from the festival."

Jack sat bolt upright. "What? You're at my *house*?"

"I'm in your *bungalow*."

Bachelor pad, thought Jack, instinctively. "What the hell? Are you *stalking* me?"

"Well, I was pissed at you for spoiling everything tonight," Sampson admitted. "Like, 'I'm Jack Sprigley, I've already been on *Bigwigs,* I can just walk away from the camera whenever I want.' It's okay for *you.* You've *had* your chance."

"What, so this is some kind of showdown? I ruined your starring role on *Bigwigs,* and so you came to my house to get revenge? Tonight was supposed to be *my* big moment!"

There was silence for a couple of seconds. Then: "Jack, I need your help."

Jack paused. There was definitely something wrong. Surely Jack was the last person someone like Sampson would ask for help?

"Something's . . . happened," he said.

"Is it my gran?" Jack pictured Marlene breaking free of her police guard, hurling hospital staff through the air with her superhuman strength, so she could reclaim by force the bungalow that was rightfully hers. He pictured her towering over Sampson, crouched in terror in the corner, and tried not to feel too gleeful at the idea. "Are my mom and my sister there?"

"It's not your gran. It's . . . Sprigley, I seriously need your help."

Jack was starting to worry now. "What the hell's going on, Sampson?"

"I can't tell you. Just come."

Jack wondered if it was some sort of trick. Was Delilah going to be there waiting for him, hidden-camera-style, for some big "gotcha" moment?

"Why can't you tell me?"

"Someone might be listening," whispered Sampson.

"Who would be listening?"

"I don't know!" said Sampson, his voice almost rising to a whinny. "Spies?"

"Spies? How old are you?"

"Just come," Sampson repeated. "I need you to fix this. I need . . ." He paused. "I need a Bigwig."

Chapter Twenty-Seven

Jack turned the corner onto his street. There was no sign of his mom's car in the driveway. There were no lights on in the house. The side walkway that led to the bungalow was cloaked in darkness.

Jack stepped on something squishy and brittle as he passed the window to his old room. He stopped, squinted, and saw that he'd trodden on a bunch of red roses wrapped in paper.

A phone lay next to the roses, its cheap plastic casing split down the side, its screen shattered. Like the flowers, it looked like it had been dropped.

Something weird was going on.

He hurried the rest of the way down the side walkway, bounded up the bungalow steps, and threw the lights on as he burst inside.

The first thing he saw was Oliver Sampson standing in the middle of the bungalow, one finger pressed to his lips, the other pointing at Jack's bed.

Lying on the bed, in a baby-blue blazer and pressed slacks, his silver hair in disarray, was Upland's mayor, Neville Perry-Moore.

For a moment Jack wondered if this was part of the Mayor for a Week deal that nobody had seen fit to tell him about. Nobody had said anything about the mayor and Jack *literally* swapping places.

Then Jack noticed the terrible black bruise around the mayor's eye.

"I think he's unconscious," whispered Sampson.

Jack closed the door and moved closer. His first thought was that his gran had attacked the mayor. First a taxi driver, then the mayor—was nobody safe from her testosterone-powered rage?

But even if that were true, it didn't go anywhere *near* explaining what Neville Perry-Moore was doing *in Jack's bed*.

"What the—? Was he like this when you got here?"

Sampson grimaced. "Not exactly."

"Wait. *You* did this? You *attacked* the mayor?"

"He was creeping around your house!"

"So were you!"

Sampson put his hand to his brow. "I . . . I thought he was a burglar or something. I didn't know it was the *mayor*. Although, technically, he's not really the mayor at the moment. Right? You are. So it's actually not as bad as it looks. Right, Sprigley?"

"What do you mean? Of course he's still the freaking mayor!" Jack realized Sampson was getting desperate. Not even Darylyn would have argued *that* technicality. He lowered his voice to a hiss. "I can't believe you *punched* the mayor in the *face*!" Jack's outrage couldn't completely eclipse the question of what the mayor had been doing at his house in the first place, but he ignored it for now.

"Don't be an idiot, Sprigley. I didn't punch him. He hit his head on the wall after I tackled him."

"Oh. Well. That's probably fine, then. I'm sure the courts won't consider it assault if it was just a *tackle*."

The mention of assault turned Sampson even paler. "But it wasn't my fault! It was an accident! I didn't think, I just . . ." He looked distressed. "I don't know my own strength."

You've had two years of living in that fully-equipped man-body, thought Jack. *Plenty of time to get to know your strength.*

"What was he doing here, anyway?" said Sampson. "And why did he have *flowers* with him?"

Jack gasped. Suddenly the penny dropped. The roses. The smashed phone. "Oh my God," he said. He turned to Sampson, not quite believing that the words he was about to utter could be true. But it all made sense.

The texting. The secrecy.

"This is going to sound crazy," he said slowly, "but I think the mayor came here to see my *gran*. I think . . ." He groaned with distaste. "Oh my God, I think this was . . . a *booty call*."

Sampson screwed his face up. "Come off it, Sprigley."

Jack wondered how long it had been going on for. Was this their first date? Or had they arranged other secret hook-ups—here, under the very roof that Jack's *Bigwigs* winnings had helped pay for? Jack felt sick at the thought.

Fortunately, Jack was spared the trauma of imagining their covert, under-the-covers activities in more detail. His thoughts were interrupted by a knock at the door and the sound of voices outside.

Sampson looked panicked. "It's the cops!"

"Jack?" came Vivi's voice through the door.

Jack did his best to stay calm. The fewer witnesses to the fact that Sampson had accidentally assaulted the mayor, the better. But then again, having Vivi standing outside calling his name was only going to attract attention.

He threw open the door and saw Vivi, Reese, Darylyn,

and Philo on the doorstep. They looked as relieved to see Jack as Jack was to see them.

"We've been texting you and calling you for the last half hour!" said Vivi.

Jack hadn't checked his phone since Sampson's distress call. He looked now and saw a bunch of messages and missed calls on the screen.

He looked out again at the four faces on the doorstep of the bungalow and took a deep breath. "You guys better come inside," he said.

Vivi and the others piled through the door and stood in the middle of Jack's bachelor pad, staring slack-jawed at the unconscious form of Mayor Neville Perry-Moore.

"Dude," said Reese, after many seconds had passed. "Why have you kidnapped the mayor?"

Jack glanced at Sampson, who was frantically chewing his nails.

"I guess this explains why nobody could contact him after you bailed on the festival, Jack," said Darylyn, wide-eyed.

"Vivi stood in as mayor for the whole thing!" said Philo.

"What the hell happened here?" said Vivi.

Jack had a sudden realization. "Holy crap. Delilah. She didn't follow you here, did she?" The last thing he needed was for any evidence of Sampson's accidental assault of the mayor to end up on camera.

Vivi glanced at Darylyn, Reese, and Philo. "Don't worry," she said, grinning. "We took care of Delilah. It was kind of like a *Bigwigs* team challenge, wasn't it, guys?"

"Oh, great," said Sampson, hands tucked under his arms to keep from chewing off his fingers entirely. "*Everyone's* a Bigwig now except me. Meanwhile, what are we going to do about *this*?"

"You still haven't explained what 'this' is!" said Vivi. "And by the way, *Sampson*, we're onto you. Philo told us the things you've been saying to Jack."

Sampson and Jack swapped glances.

"In the locker room," said Vivi.

Jack shrugged. He really wanted to avoid a situation where anyone might be tempted to use the words "baldy-balls." "Yeah, I'm not sure we really need to—"

"So what?" said Sampson. "He *is* a baldy-balls."

There it is, thought Jack.

Reese glared at Sampson. "Dude. Watch it."

Jack held his hands out diplomatically. "Guys. Calm down. It's just one of those nicknames like when you call a person with red hair 'Bluey.' Or when you call a really tall person 'Shorty.' When Sampson says 'baldy-balls,' what he really means is 'Jack has a much higher than average quantity of pubi—'"

"Marleeeeeeeeeeeeeeeene . . . ?"

Everyone spun around. The mayor was stirring into consciousness.

"Let's get out of here!" hissed Sampson.

Vivi frowned. "Did he say 'Marlene'?" She turned to Jack. "As in your *gran* Marlene?"

"Where—where am I?" groaned Mayor Perry-Moore. He squinted at Jack and the others in turn, gathering energy like an Egyptian mummy being slowly revived by dark sorcery. "Am I going crazy, or did somebody *attack* me?"

Jack's mind raced. There was a chance the mayor would recognize Sampson. He might press charges. Anything could happen. They could all end up as accomplices. He had to think quick.

The mayor's gaze drew ever closer to Sampson.

Suddenly Jack realized. There was a chance he could save the situation. He lunged for the open drawer in his dresser, hoping the thing he was looking for was there.

It was. It was always there. It always turned up, somehow.

Jack whisked the merkin from the drawer and slapped it onto Sampson's chin.

Sampson staggered back, clawing at his face. "What the—?"

"It's a disguise!" Jack hissed. "Go with it!"

Philo frowned, and went to raise his hand. "Um—"

"Not now!" said Jack.

Mayor Perry-Moore squinted at Sampson. "You. You with the beard."

Jack grabbed Sampson by the wrists.

"It's okay, he's just a burglar. A big old beardy burglar. We caught him in the act, didn't we, guys? Citizens' arrest. We just have to get this hairy bad guy down to the police station. We saw everything, we can give a statement, no need for you to get involved, Mr. Mayor, sir."

"Jack *Sprigley*? Is that you?" As he said it, Mayor Perry-Moore seemed to remember where he was. His cheeks reddened slightly, and a guilty, worried look crept onto his face.

Sampson, meanwhile, struggled free of Jack's not-exactly-iron grip. His nose twitched and he screwed up his face. "What the hell is this *made* from?"

"Um—"

"Shut *up*, Philo!"

Sampson sneezed. The merkin unglued itself from his face and fell onto the floor.

The mayor's eyes grew huge. "That's no burglar! I remember now!" He winced in pain. "One of you, help me up!"

Reese and Darylyn rushed forward and grabbed the mayor under his arms, helping him swivel out of bed.

"I'm going straight to the police," he said. "I'm old college buddies with the superintendent. We play golf every week. Sweet *Lord*, my head hurts."

Vivi glanced at Jack, and then they both glanced at Sampson.

"Assault and battery," said Mayor Perry-Moore, clutching the side of his head. "Assault and battery against a city official! What's your name?"

Sampson stuck his chin out stubbornly. "Like I have to answer *your* questions. What were *you* doing sneaking around the Sprigleys' house?"

"His name's Oliver Sampson," said Philo helpfully.

Reese glared at him. "Dude!"

"Oliver Sampson," said the mayor. "Your parents, are they the Sampsons with the vineyard at Doubleknee Bend?"

"M-maybe," said Sampson.

"They are," Philo cheerfully confirmed.

"Dude!"

"Well," said the mayor, "you won't be picking grapes this summer, that's for damn sure. Picking up rubbish, maybe. That's if you get away with a community service order. More likely you're looking at a summer in juvenile detention!"

Everyone gasped.

Juvenile detention? thought Jack. In a way, it seemed a good fit for Sampson. He'd probably be top dog in the jailhouse before too long, just like he was king of the locker room at school.

Sampson went ashen-faced. But a second later the chin

was back out again, and he'd puffed his chest out along with it. "Y-yeah? W-well, I'd like to see you try."

"I won't need to try," said Mayor Perry-Moore. "I'm the biggest man in town! I can do anything!"

"Including creeping around taxpayers' houses at eight p.m. on a Friday night?" said Vivi.

Mayor Perry-Moore opened and closed his mouth. "It's . . . it's a new part of the Mayor for a Week program. A surprise one-on-one meet-and-greet from the real mayor while the junior mayor takes over."

Sampson snorted. "As if. Tell everyone what you figured out, Sprigley."

Jack glanced at the others. The mayor looked flustered. "The only thing you ought to be figuring out is how long you want to spend in detention! Because you're all involved in this. Every one of you. He might be the ringleader"—he glared at Sampson—"but you're *all* culpable."

They were back to outbigging each other, Jack realized. Sampson and the mayor, both frightened and embarrassed. Both trying to hide it by being the bigger man.

"What about *you*?" said Sampson. "Sprigley here could have you arrested for trespassing if he wanted to. Couldn't you, Sprigley?"

"Trespassing? I'm not a trespasser! I'm the blooming *mayor*! I can do what I like. And that includes locking thugs like you away for the rest of your junior high school years, if you're not careful!"

The situation was getting out of hand. Jack needed to think of something to defuse it, fast. And then the solution came to him in a flash of brilliance.

"You've got it wrong," said Jack loudly.

Everyone turned to look at him. Jack looked at Sampson and then at Vivi. He took a deep breath and stepped forward, eyes locked with Upland's five-time mayor, Neville Perry-Moore.

"Sampson wasn't the one who attacked you."

He stuck out his chin and his chest.

"It was me."

Chapter Twenty-Eight

Mayor Perry-Moore frowned. "What did you say?"

"That's right," said Jack. He jabbed at his own unconvincing excuse for a chest with his thumb. "It was *me* who knocked you over. I found out about you and my gran sexting each other and I was super pissed about it."

Vivi and the others swapped confused (and slightly grossed-out) glances.

Jack swallowed nervously. Somehow he didn't think juvenile detention would be quite as easy for him as it would for Sampson. Junior high was hard enough.

"So . . . ," Jack went on. "So I was all, like, 'Yeah, I'm going to smack that old manwhore across the head!'" He flashed Neville Perry-Moore his meanest glare. "I took you *down*, yo!"

The mayor looked Jack up and down. "You? Don't be ridiculous. You're . . . you're so *small*."

Bingo, thought Jack. It was exactly the reaction he'd wanted.

"Yeah, and I *still* took you down. 'There's Neville Perry-Moore,' they'll say. 'He might've been the big man in town once upon a time, but then he let himself get smacked down by a *kid*.' I mean, dude . . . I haven't even got *pubes* yet."

There were gasps. (Not-very-shocked gasps, Jack couldn't help noticing.)

"So, sure," he said. "Press charges if you want. That is, if you want everyone in town knowing you couldn't even defend yourself against pubeless Jack *Sprigley*. In which case: I'll see *you* in *court*!"

There was an awkward silence.

"*O-o-o-r,*" said Vivi, side-eying Jack, "*another* reason you might not want to press charges, Mr. Mayor, is that your 'special lady friend' might not be so eager to swap texts with the man who sent her grandson to jail?"

Right, thought Jack. *Clearly a far superior tactic.* Which meant he'd just confessed to being a pubeless freak in front of everyone for nothing. "Y-yeah," he said. "That, too."

Mayor Perry-Moore glared at Vivi for a moment with narrowed eyes. Jack held his breath.

"Well," said the mayor eventually, "maybe I *was* a little hasty. But don't think you're completely off the hook. You might be able to throw a lucky punch, but it's obvious that you still have a *lot* of growing up to do."

"Hmm," said Darylyn, cocking her head slightly. "That alarm you can hear? That would be the Hypocrisy Scale hitting the big ten point oh."

Jack relaxed a little. Darylyn was right. Mayor Perry-Moore had just demonstrated his distinct lack of maturity in the way he handled the whole situation—but at least he'd stopped talking about pressing charges.

Sampson, meanwhile, was looking at Jack in complete awe of what had just happened. Not that Jack had long to savor it. The mayor pushed past him and was hobbling out of the bungalow.

Reese reached after him. "Dude, are you sure you're okay?"

"I'm fine," he grumbled. "I fell off the Ferris wheel at the opening of Raisin World World and lived to tell the tale. I think I can cope with a black eye. I'm a man." He drew himself up as tall as he could. "A red-blooded, stouthearted *man*."

Vivi took out her phone. "We'll call you a taxi."

"Yes, please," whimpered Mayor Perry-Moore. He limped gingerly down the bungalow steps and along the side walkway to the front of the house.

Jack and Vivi and the others followed after him.

"Nice work, stepping in to save Sampson's butt," Vivi whispered.

"Yeah," said Jack. He glanced back at Sampson, who was dawdling behind them, looking sheepish. "I thought I'd finally found a way of making the 'late bloomer' thing pay off. Your plan was better."

Vivi shrugged. "Better. But not as brave. Anyway, he never would have pressed charges. Not unless he was willing to explain to the police what he was doing at your house."

Reese leaned over to Jack. "Dude. *Sexting?* Really?"

Jack nodded. "Being a weirdo pervert runs in the family, I guess."

"You're not *that* much of a weirdo pervert," said Darylyn.

It was one of the nicest things anyone had said to Jack in a long time.

Philo frowned at his phone. "This stupid thing doesn't even *have* a sexting button."

Ahead of them, the mayor paused briefly at the window to Jack's old room. It was dark inside. Jack figured his mom and Hallie were still at the hospital, dealing with the fallout from Marlene's hormonal rampage.

Vivi reached down and picked up the roses Jack had trodden on earlier. Jack picked up the smashed phone, then turned to the mayor. "Why *were* you sneaking around out here, anyway?"

Mayor Perry-Moore reached out for the crushed flowers, staring sadly at them for a moment. "Marlene and I were supposed to meet at the river for a moonlight picnic. We've been texting and talking for months, ever since I came and spoke at one of her retirees' lunches. But she never arrived. She's been so *unlike* herself lately. Typing her messages in capital letters, that kind of thing."

Philo nodded. "It was probably the side effects. You know, from the tes—"

Jack was about to tackle Philo to the ground when the side walkway was flooded with light as a car pulled into the driveway. The sound of the car engine rumbled away into silence and the headlights flicked off. Jack's eyes adjusted to the darkness again.

It was his mom's car. With his gran in the front passenger seat.

Jack and the others spilled out of the side walkway and into the carport. Mayor Perry-Moore limped out after them.

"Mom!" said Jack. "Gran!"

"Marlene!" the mayor cried.

Adele stepped out of the car, looking exhausted. Marlene

sat frozen for a moment, a bandage on her forehead, her hair sticking out in all directions.

She looked like a lipsticked werewolf on the morning after a full moon.

"Jack? Shouldn't you be at the festival?" Adele noticed the mayor standing next to Jack and the others. "Wait a minute, why is—?"

But before Adele could say anything more, Marlene had burst out of the car like a freshly cuffed perp trying to make a break for it. She'd seen the mayor too—and was tearing straight toward him.

"No!" Jack cried.

Marlene pounced on Mayor Perry-Moore in what seemed to be a doomed attempt to wrap her legs around his waist. His legs instantly buckled underneath him and they both toppled over. The mayor's skull was about to hit a solid object for the second time that night when Sampson caught him under the arms and lifted the writhing mass of geriatric lust upright. Marlene snapped back to reality and clambered down from Mayor Perry-Moore again.

Adele looked on in shock. "Is someone going to explain why *the mayor* is at our house? And why my mother has just attempted to *grind* him?"

Another flood of headlights washed over them all as a bright-green hatchback pulled into the driveway. Nats and

Hallie got out. Jack swallowed nervously. Here he was, face-to-face again with the girl he'd hoped to fool the world into thinking was his girlfriend.

"Oh my God," said Hallie. "Is that *Mayor Perry-Moore?*"

Jack racked his brains, trying to think of a clever lie to tell his mom and Hallie about why the mayor had visited Gran—some innocent explanation that would spare Marlene and the mayor from having to confess to their telephonic tryst. Because you weren't supposed to be sexting at seventy. Just like you weren't supposed to be pubeless at fourteen.

"Things don't always happen when they're supposed to," said Jack, shrugging. He turned to Marlene and Mayor Perry-Moore. "You should tell her."

"I can't deal with this," said Adele. "Whatever's going on, I don't want to know about it. I've just had to convince a taxi driver not to press charges against my mother for nearly breaking his arm."

"I thought he was attacking me."

"He was helping you into the taxi." Adele glanced at the roses Mayor Perry-Moore was holding. Her eyes grew wide. "Mom, have you been secretly *dating* the mayor?"

Mayor Perry-Moore put a hand on Marlene's shoulder. Jack wasn't sure if he was trying to lend her the strength to be honest, or just trying to keep himself steady after the onset of a mild concussion.

Marlene looked up at the mayor, then turned and reached out toward her daughter.

"Adele," she said. "Love. We didn't . . . I just didn't think it was fair. For me to be happy. When you . . ."

Adele covered her mouth with her hand. "I am happy," she insisted.

Marlene shuffled forward and took Adele in her arms.

Jack relaxed. Everything was out in the open. Everyone could start behaving like grown-ups.

Or at least pretend to.

Chapter Twenty-Nine

he next day of the Fourteenth Annual Upland Hot-Air Balloon Festival dawned with a balloon flight over Lake Meridian. Four-wheel drives and minibuses were parked at the terminus of the access road, just beyond the shore. Half a dozen balloons were already in the air, ready to catch the first light of the new day.

Jack and the others had arrived earlier in near darkness, taking a shuttle bus together from the Ninth Street Mall. As the dawn lightened, the spindly silhouettes of the scrub trees at the edge of the lake took form against the backdrop of a blue morning sky.

It had been Delilah's idea to film the morning balloon

ride to replace the failed balloon race of the night before. She said they could fudge the details and splice it into yesterday's footage, and no one would ever know the difference. But Jack and Sampson had refused to rerun the race for the cameras. They would ride in one balloon, together. Delilah had taken some convincing—it wasn't the big ending she'd been expecting. To be fair, it wasn't exactly the ending Jack had been expecting either.

Sampson and Philo were the first to climb aboard the balloon. It was, Jack noted with relief, a balloon that sported the traditional reverse-teardrop shape, as opposed to looking like a pair of shriveled grapes or an overblown rocket ship emblazoned with bulging avocados.

There seemed to be little danger of mistaking this balloon's alternating light-green and dark-green stripes for the furrows and grooves of a giant scrotum.

Reese and Darylyn climbed in after Sampson and Philo. The balloon operator sent a few blasts of heated air up into the balloon.

Vivi turned to Jack. "You go first."

Jack shook his head. "No. I've done too much cutting ahead lately. After you."

"I insist."

"So do I."

Vivi sighed. "Look, let's just get on board. Everyone else

is in there already. Why are we arguing about this?"

In the end, Jack went last. He put his foot into the lowest of the zigzagged rungs cut into the side of the basket. Reese, Philo, and Sampson helped him over the edge.

As the balloon pilot got ready for takeoff, Jack glanced back to the shore. Delilah and her crew looked bleary-eyed and pasty-faced. This was the last piece of filming on their schedule before they flew out of Upland.

Delilah went to tap something into her phone, then screwed up her face in disgust, as though she couldn't bring herself to even touch the screen.

Jack couldn't help smirking to himself. Part of the reason Delilah was so reluctant about the ending to Jack's *Bigwigs* story was that she was still mad about what had happened the evening before. When he'd stormed away from the balloon festival, Delilah's first instinct had apparently been to go after Jack and chase the drama. But Vivi, Reese, and Darylyn knew the score now. They knew Delilah had set Jack and Sampson up against each other. Why she'd done it, they weren't sure. They'd just known that the last thing Jack needed at that moment was more *Bigwigs*.

Reese had acted first. Noticing that Todd was wearing a Twisted Antlers T-shirt, he managed to hold the crew up for at least ten minutes by launching into an intense discussion about Scandinavian death metal.

Then Vivi, up on the bandstand giving the launch speech, went off script and told everyone at the festival that Delilah and her crew were filming a documentary called *Fifteen Minutes of Me*. Anyone who wanted to be on camera could go up and talk about themselves for fifteen minutes.

A crowd circled the camera immediately, trapping Brett like a lone survivor in a zombie movie.

When Delilah took out her phone, apparently determined to get her footage any way she could, Philo whisked it out of her hand and—for reasons known only to Philo—dashed off into the crowd with the phone stuffed down the front of his pants.

Eventually, as the opening night wound down, Delilah had gotten her crew back. She'd gotten her phone back too—still operational despite the slightly more-humid-than-recommended environment it had just been subjected to. Delilah had apparently threatened to follow Vivi and the others to Jack's house when Darylyn gave her the deadliest of deadly Darylyn looks and stopped her in her tracks. "You've messed with Jack enough, lady," she said. "We're his friends. Only we get to do that. Now *back off*."

And so Delilah backed off, and Delilah backed down.

After everything that had happened, Jack wasn't sure he deserved to have everyone looking out for him like that.

He'd been the opposite of loyal to Vivi, but still they hadn't ditched him.

Maybe there'd never been any danger of that in the first place.

Jack had imagined the takeoff would be a slow and steady rise into the sky, but it wasn't like that. It wasn't like they were suddenly launched into the atmosphere, either, though. What seemed to happen was that one moment they could feel the ground beneath them, and the next it was gone. When it happened, it took Jack a second to realize they were even airborne.

Jack joined the others at the edge of the basket. Dozens more balloons had lifted off from the ground, all at different altitudes, all sharing the same lifting urge, the same surrender to the wind.

Jack forgot himself for a moment. He wasn't Jack the Mayor for a Week, or Jack the Bigwig, or even Jack the pubeless weirdo freak-boy. The world suddenly seemed vast and full of possibility. He felt, for that moment at least, the freedom not to be anything or anyone at all.

Just then, Jack remembered something. He reached into his pocket and pulled something out with a short laugh. Everyone turned to look at him.

"Dude," said Reese. "Why did you bring that grody fake beard with you?"

Vivi and Darylyn looked disturbed. Sampson instinctively reached up and scratched his chin as if bothered by fleas.

"It's not a beard," said Philo. "It's—"

"It's something I don't need anymore," said Jack. Then he stopped and looked serious for a moment. "Not that I ever did."

In truth, with everything that had been going on, he realized he'd forgotten to do his usual pube check the past couple of mornings.

When he was sure the balloon operator wasn't looking, Jack tossed the merkin over the side of the basket.

It seemed to hover in the air for a moment, like a particularly disgusting species of albatross, then disappeared from sight.

Delilah and her crew had driven around to the other side of the lake to film the landing. After the descent to the lakeshore, Jack and the others climbed out, still buzzing from the flight.

Jack looked along the shore to where other balloons were starting to land. He blinked as a familiar balloon made its descent.

It was the Raisin World balloon, hanging in the sky like a giant pair of testicles.

It landed on the shore, and out of its basket climbed a party of men, young and old, whooping and high-fiving and bear-hugging one another, all ruggedly dressed in khakis and lumberjack shirts and other wilderness gear. It was only when Jack spotted Mr. Trench among them, breaking free of a bear hug with another member of the group, that he realized these were the Lionheart Tigerwolves.

Jack laughed incredulously. The Lionheart Tigerwolves had somehow ended up flying over Lake Meridian suspended beneath an airborne scrotum. It was almost too good to be true.

"Jack Sprigley!" Mr. Trench's voice rang out across the lake as he spotted Jack and rushed over. He slapped Jack on the shoulders. "This is an unexpected rendezvous! What an experience, eh? Do you know, I've never actually flown before!"

"In a hot-air balloon?"

"In anything!"

Jack frowned. "Not even in, like, an army helicopter or something?"

"Good heavens, no! But we all had such a great time up there, we're going to fly straight back over the lake again!"

"That balloon . . . ," Jack began. "It's kind of—"

"Isn't it marvelous! I can't explain it, but as soon as we saw it, we all thought, 'Yes, that's the one for us!'" Mr. Trench waved back at the other Lionheart Tigerwolves.

With that, Mr. Trench slapped Jack on the shoulders again and hurried back to the scrotum-shaped balloon formerly known as Hot-Air Force One.

"Imagine not realizing that you're attached to a giant scrotum," Jack said to Vivi, shaking his head.

"Yeah," said Vivi wryly. "Almost as embarrassing as telling everyone you've been masturbating for two weeks straight." She paused. "I think the word you're looking for is 'touché.'"

Jack smiled. "Touché," he said. He was relieved to see Vivi smile back.

Jack wandered over to where Delilah was standing next to the minivan. "You look happier than before," he said.

"Just relieved you made a safe landing," said Delilah. "And so do you, by the way. Look happier, I mean."

Jack glanced back at Sampson and the others. "I guess I'm just glad this *Bigwigs* thing is nearly over." He looked Delilah in the eye. "It didn't turn out the way I thought it would."

Delilah crossed her arms and stared down at her feet for a moment. "Listen, Jack. I shouldn't have played Sampson against you. I'm sorry about that. But that's what we do. We try to make stories out of ordinary life." She looked into the distance, then turned back to Jack. "I have friends who work on big shows, important shows. And here's me, working on this kids' thing. So I pitched the reunion idea. Get the past contestants back, add a bit of drama, make it feel older and cooler. And then, when I saw the weird vibe between you and Oliver, and found out he'd been *rejected* from the show . . . I guess I got carried away trying to make things out to be bigger than they were."

"I get it," said Jack. "It's not like I've been totally up-front this whole time either. I've been meaning to ask about the Bigwigs Board thing, though. I didn't get to have my big moment opening the festival on camera. Because of the whole storming-off-like-a-not-very-manly-diva thing. Is that . . . going to be a problem?"

"You still want to be in the running?"

Jack thought for a moment. "I don't know," he said, finally. He wasn't sure he was up for the competition anymore.

"But you'll still do the reunion, right? I mean, I don't want to play hardball or anything, but you did sign a contract. You're still technically required to appear on the reunion show."

Jack didn't answer right away. He still had to do the bit he was dreading most—stand up onstage with the other Bigwigs in front of a studio audience and try to look as though he'd grown up as much as the rest of them, when it was obvious that he hadn't.

If puberty doesn't happen soon, thought Jack, *it's probably time to go see a doctor or something.* Or, failing that, dip into the half-used jar of testosterone cream he'd stashed in his bathroom after all the drama of the night before.

In the meantime, could he do it? Could he really stand onstage with the other Bigwigs?

He looked back at Vivi and Reese and Darylyn, at Philo and Sampson.

Reunions, he thought.

Reunions he was up for.

A week later . . .

"Coming soon on the new season of Bigwigs *. . ."*

(Fade in to a dimly lit stage. Four spotlights beam down into empty space.)

"It's been two years since we crowned our first Bigwigs *champion. We've seen scores of hopefuls take to this same stage, seeking glory. There have been challenges. There have been triumphs."*

(Dramatic music.)

"There have been bitter defeats."

(Quick montage of the new Bigwigs*. The next generation.)*

"Soon, a brand-new cast joins us for our third year of ups and downs in the Bigwigs *Mansion. And this year,* Bigwigs *gets even bigger. You've seen our contestants take on challenges in the grown-up world. You've seen them sent off to work for some of the toughest bosses in the country. But this year, the tables are*

turned. *This time, the Bigwigs are calling the shots. This time, it could be your boss getting performance reviewed . . ."*

(Dramatic boom)

" . . . by a twelve-year-old."

(The words "twelve-year-old" echo annoyingly in surround sound stereo.)

"But that's not all. We've got a special surprise in store for Bigwigs *fans in our season premiere."*

(Another quick montage: Piers Blain, Hope Chanders, Amit Gondra, Jack Sprigley, Mickey Santini, Denny Trimble, Cassie Tau. Quick bursts of YouTube videos, talk-show appearances, crowds screaming at in-store promotions—then a mysterious cut to a sky full of hot-air balloons . . .)

"See which familiar faces we've brought back—and who we're bringing back for good!—on the new season of Bigwigs. *Next Sunday at seven."*

(Fade out.)

Chapter Thirty

Jack's mom let the engine run. "You're sure you don't want me to pick you up?" she asked.

Jack unbuckled his seat belt. They were parked at the top of the long, winding driveway that climbed the hill above Doubleknee Bend. Rows of vines stretched out below them. "It's fine," he said. "Sampson's going to call a taxi for us. Plus: getting picked up by your mom. It's not very manly."

His mom frowned.

"I'm joking," said Jack.

"Good. Because I was pretty sure we'd gotten over this stupid 'man of the house' stuff. I've told you—there's no one person who has to look after everything." His mom gripped the steering wheel tighter, as if the car were suddenly in danger of rolling back down the hill. "There might be a huge hole right in the middle of us, but we can do this together. Okay?"

Jack nodded. "So . . . about Gran and the mayor . . . ," he said after a moment. "How are you feeling about *that*?"

"How do I feel? How do I *feel*? *It's as weird as f—*" She caught Jack staring wide-eyed at her and held the *f* for five full seconds before concluding with a timid "—udge." "But I can't pretend it's not happening. It turns out that's *not* such a great solution." She paused, then switched the ignition off. "You know, Hallie was pretty disappointed we're not all going to be home watching the big show together."

A week ago, Jack wouldn't have believed that. Hallie had *never* watched *Bigwigs*, not even when Jack had been a contestant. *Especially* not then, actually. And now he could kind of understand why. Back during the excitement of that first season, Hallie had been the same age Jack was now. There'd been no TV cameras pointed at her, no spotlight or special attention. Instead, their mom had gotten swept up in twelve-year-old Jack's *Bigwigs* success as the finals had gotten closer and closer.

And just like Jack, Hallie must have missed their dad like crazy. As much as she was the big sister, she was only ten when he died. It didn't take a genius to figure out how crappy it would have felt, with Adele letting herself get too wrapped up in Jack's stupid *Bigwigs* stuff to give Hallie the attention she needed.

Anyway, Hallie's usual icy attitude toward Jack was showing signs of thawing. After he'd gotten home from the dawn balloon flight earlier in the week, he'd gone to apologize to her for the whole business with Nats. She hadn't even slammed her door in his face, or hurled so much as a single bobby pin in his eyes.

"Sorry?" she'd said. "Why are you sorry?"

"For getting in the way of you and Nats becoming besties," said Jack. "For luring her away with my promises of fame and stardom."

Hallie had smirked. "Yeah, I think you might be giving yourself a *little* too much credit there, Mr. Showbiz. Despite what I usually say, it's not *always* about you. But in fact, I think you might actually have done some good for once. Now that Nats has given up on a TV career, she's more like . . . I don't know, a real person, I guess."

"Wait, Nats said she doesn't want to be on TV anymore?"

Hallie nodded.

"Why?"

"I don't know, exactly. Maybe you should ask her."

"Really?" said Jack. "You'd be okay with that?"

Hallie had shrugged and pulled out her phone. "Need her number?"

Jack had tried to look nonchalant. "Already got it." Then he remembered wiping it after bailing on the festival. "Wait! I deleted it." He gave a knowing smile. "Lovers' tiff."

Hallie rolled her eyes. "Oh God."

Jack had texted Nats later that day. To his surprise, she'd called him right back. "Jack! Don't tell me I'm speaking to you live from the *Bigwigs* studio?"

When Jack had told her the filming for the reunion episode was still a few days away, Nats had asked him if he was feeling nervous. The truth was, he wasn't sure *what* he felt. He hadn't seen the footage Delilah had cut together at that point. Until he saw that, he wouldn't know if he'd succeeded in turning himself into the man he'd wanted everyone to think he was.

Not that he was too worried about measuring up to the other Bigwigs anymore. Or anyone else. He was more worried about measuring up to the Jack he'd been before.

"Anyway, it wasn't *Bigwigs* I wanted to talk to you about," said Jack. "I wanted to apologize. For the whole 'fake girlfriend' thing. Vivi was right. I was kind of treating you like a prize, instead of an actual person."

There was silence on the other end of the line.

"Hallie says you're giving up on the TV host dream?" said Jack, wondering if she was still there.

"Not giving it up, exactly," said Nats after a moment. "More like, giving it second thoughts. Actually, I'm kind of glad I never got my big moment on camera at the festival."

"Again," insisted Jack, "*really* sorry about that whole thing. I know how embarrassing it would have been, pretending to be going out with an eighth grader and having it recorded *on film*."

"No," said Nats. "It's not that. I mean, yes, obviously that would have made me a total laughingstock—"

(*Could have given that a little sugarcoating,* thought Jack.)

"But the thing is, Jack, once people see you a certain way, it turns out it's pretty hard to convince them you're actually something else. If I do end up on TV, I want to make sure it's the *real* Nats that people are seeing. Not the fake one."

The next day, when Delilah had Skyped Jack to show him the package she was putting together, Nats's words had still been echoing in his head.

Jack realized his mom was still talking to him.

"You'd better get a move on," she said, getting ready to turn the keys again. "It's nearly seven o'clock."

Jack sat there for a moment, not moving. "It's weird. He probably never thought I'd end up being on TV, like him."

"Your dad?"

Jack nodded. "He never got to see me turn into who I am now."

"No. But the Jack you are now isn't so different from the Jack you were then. And I think you've already figured out that's not such a bad thing."

Jack collected himself, then slid out of the car with a snack-laden backpack slung over his shoulder and a large brown paper gift bag in his hand. "Thanks for the ride," he said. He shut the door, poked his head through the open window, and, with a goofy look on his face, added, "Enjoy the big show!"

His mom narrowed her eyes. "You haven't told them, have you?"

Jack didn't answer.

Chapter Thirty-One

ampson had dragged an old couch and some beanbags into the garage and set them up in front of the big-screen TV. The garage had been his bedroom for the past two years. He'd been banished from the house when his early growth spurt had hit, like a monster locked away in a dungeon.

Vivi, Reese, and Darylyn were on the couch, haggling over the pizza menu. Philo poured Raisin World Sparkling Soda into plastic cups.

"That's a Skyhawk Gladiator," said Sampson, pointing to a model fighter jet with a pair of giant torpedoes bolted beneath its wings. The model sat on a shelf in an old metal locker, along with dozens of other planes, cars, and tanks, all painstakingly painted and assembled.

"These are really good," said Jack.

"Thanks," said Sampson. "That was what I wrote down on my *Bigwigs* application. 'Model skills.' But I had to stop building them after . . . you know." He held up his hands. "Couldn't get through a single kit without snapping a wing or busting an axle." He paused. "That's why I never made it onto *Bigwigs*, I think. They must have taken one look at my photos and decided I looked too old."

Jack thought back to the start of seventh grade, when all the guys in the locker room had gazed up at Sampson in awe. Except he was starting to understand that maybe it didn't feel like that to Sampson. All Sampson would have felt was *different*.

Jack glanced back at the others, who were still yanking the pizza menu back and forth and arguing passionately on the subject of anchovies. "I haven't told anyone this," said Jack. "But when I got sent home from *Bigwigs* in the first week of the finals? It wasn't because Hope Chanders got more ringtone downloads than I did. They flat-out told me. They said I wasn't 'right.'"

"What does that mean?"

Jack shrugged. "I guess they already knew who they wanted. Because it wasn't just about *Bigwigs*: It was about everything that comes after. They wanted someone who could be the face of *Bigwigs* forever. Someone not too old, but not too young, either. Someone who'd 'grown' as a contestant, so they had a story to tell."

Sampson shook his head. "Neither of us ever stood a chance." He checked his watch. "Okay, time to log on to the forum. Part of the whole preshow ritual. By the way, thanks for not telling the others about those stupid posts I made. And, also, thanks for not getting too pissed about all those stupid posts I made."

"Didn't take any notice," said Jack with a shrug. "Though if it wasn't for those posts on the forum, I probably wouldn't have found out you'd been rejected from *Bigwigs*, so I probably wouldn't have signed on for the reunion show and been a jerk to lots of people and had a pair of giant testicles dangled in front of my face with the whole town watching. But whatever."

Sampson nodded absentmindedly. "Cool," he said, then went to find his laptop.

"Look at you two, best of friends all of a sudden."

Jack turned to see Vivi standing behind him. In her hands was a pair of plastic cups full of Philo's fizzy purple liquid.

"This stuff is gross, by the way," she said, handing him a cup.

"Speaking of gross," said Jack, taking a sniff, "that's pretty much how I've been acting lately. Especially to you. Which is why . . ." Jack opened up the brown gift bag he'd been holding on to since he arrived, and reached inside. "Just some civic regalia. To say sorry."

He handed Vivi a set of mayoral robes. He'd had them made by the same seamstress Delilah had used to sew Jack's and Sampson's balloons for the festival—but he'd made sure to be very, *very* specific about the design.

"You were right," he said. "I totally stole Mayor for a Week from you. And it was selfish. And self-serving. And backstabbing. All true."

Vivi laughed and pulled the robes over her head. "I love them! I should have worn these to the luncheon." She must have noticed Jack looking confused. "The Mayor for a Week luncheon?" she said. "I didn't realize, but Natsumi Distagio does this thing each year where she hires out a room in one of her dad's restaurants and invites all the past Mayors for a Week." She paused. "I just figured you weren't there because you'd already flown down to film the *Bigwigs* thing."

"Oh yeah," said Jack. "Totally. Bummed I couldn't make it. But, you know. Already had my hands full. . . ."

Vivi brushed down her new mayoral robes. "I think I might've misjudged Nats, actually. Turns out it was *her* idea to have an essay competition to choose the Mayor for a Week this year. She felt like it was all too much of a popularity contest. I think I probably owe her an apology." She looked up at Jack. "And while we're talking apologies . . . there's one other thing you haven't said sorry for."

"What's that?"

Vivi fixed him with a stare. "Ditching me over the break."

Jack opened and closed his mouth like a goldfish who's just heard something particularly astonishing. "Wait—what? I didn't ditch *you*! You guys all ditched *me*!"

"Well, yeah, Reese and Darylyn were always going to drop off the radar, once it was obvious they'd hooked up."

"Yes," said Jack. "That . . . obvious thing that happened." He paused. "So when did you figure that out, exactly?"

"Hmm . . . halfway through last semester, maybe?"

"Oh," said Jack, doing his best to look surprised and sympathetic. "That late, huh? I guess I *am* pretty good at picking up on these things. . . ."

"So that wasn't why you were avoiding me over the break, then? I thought you might have been . . . worried."

"Worried about what?"

"That . . . everyone would make the obvious assumption?"

Jack looked at her blankly.

Vivi rolled her eyes. "You know. Four of us. Four divides into two pairs. Reese and Darylyn make one pair, so . . ."

Jack felt his cheeks turn red. All he managed to say was "Um"—and even that took him a few attempts.

Vivi shrugged. "But then we had that chat in homeroom when school came back and it turned out we were all cool with the way things were, and then Sampson started hanging out with us and four became five, and you can't divide five into pairs, so the numbers didn't point so obviously to . . . you know. All *that* stuff."

"That stuff," said Jack, nodding in furious agreement.

"Which is something I'm *definitely* not ready for," said Vivi firmly.

"S-o-o-o-o not ready," said Jack. "I mean, if you measured how ready I am for that stuff, I'd be, like, *zero* percent ready. I guess what I'm saying is, if the standard unit of measurement for that stuff was, like, *pubes*? I'd be a *total* baldy-balls. In terms of readiness. For that stuff."

Vivi frowned. "You know that's a *really* weird thing to measure *anything* by, right?"

Jack grinned. "I'm starting to realize that, yeah."

"Dudes!" Reese called out. "It's starting!"

The frenzied blare of the preshow commercial break gave way to the blaring frenzy of the new *Bigwigs* intro. Everyone gathered around the TV.

Jack settled back on the couch next to Vivi. His heart was beating fast. The moment had finally come.

None of them knew what was about to happen. None of them seemed to have figured it out.

None of them seemed to realize they were about to see a completely different Jack.

Sampson sat perched on a pair of beanbags, laptop resting on his knees, staring openmouthed at the TV. "What the hell?"

"Dude . . . ," said Reese.

"Where *were* you?" said Vivi.

"*Bigwigs* sucks," said Darylyn.

"They cut you out!" said Sampson. "They completely cut you out!"

"What are you talking about?" said Philo. "Jack won the whole thing, didn't you see? They put him on the Bigwigs Board! It all turned for the best!"

Reese turned to him. "Dude, that was *Piers Blain*."

"'WHERE WAS JACK?! WHERE WAS JACK?'" Sampson read aloud from the laptop. "Huh. At least they're not attacking me this time. Some of those emojis were *really* mean." He read from the screen again. "'Also, *Bigwigs* is all different now and we don't like it. We don't even care that our stupid parents wouldn't let us go and be in the audience. We're watching *Junior Animal Surgeons* now, which is way cooler and has horses.'"

Vivi shook her head. "I can't believe they put you through all that stress and flew you down and didn't even include you in the show. Not even a mention! Did you *know* they were going to do that?"

"Guys," said Jack. "It's all cool. I Skyped with Delilah last week, and she showed me the footage she'd been editing. They'd turned me into a completely different Jack. I looked like the biggest man in town. And that was when I decided."

The others looked at each other.

"Decided what?" said Vivi.

"That it wasn't me. That I didn't want to fake it after all. I didn't *want* to be a completely different Jack. So I pulled out. I didn't do the reunion show. I'm done with being a Bigwig."

"You *what?*" cried Sampson.

"Um, didn't you sign a contract?" said Darylyn.

"Delilah found a loophole," said Jack. "She realized there might have been a problem anyway, as soon as she saw me on Skype."

"What do you mean?" asked Vivi, looking stunned. "What problem?"

Jack's ears felt warm. "Well, she wasn't sure it would match. All the stuff we filmed. She thought people might . . . notice."

"Dude, notice what?" said Reese.

"Just that, since the start of filming, I guess I'd kind of started to . . . change?"

In retrospect, Jack thought, *I probably should have waited until after the Skype call to do the unscheduled pube check.*

But there it had been. The proof. The dash was underway. The charge had begun.

The cork had finally popped.

Jack scratched his neck nervously as the others tilted their heads and looked him up and down.

"Oh yeah," said Darylyn. "I guess so."

A less than monumental silence followed. Jack couldn't believe it.

"You didn't even *notice* that I've finally hit my growth spurt? You really *weren't* paying any attention to how far behind I was from the rest of you?"

"I was."

"Apart from Sampson?"

Reese shrugged. "Dude, we've all had our own stuff going on."

"Wait," said Vivi. "So if you didn't fly down to do the reunion show, and you didn't come to the Mayor for a Week luncheon, what exactly have you been *doing* this whole time?"

Jack paused. "Oh," he said. "Well, that's no biggie. I just took a few days off school. Things have been pretty crazy lately, so—"

"You didn't even *tell* us?" said Reese.

"Seriously," said Sampson. "You guys are *the worst* at communicating with each other."

Jack held his hands out defensively. "Guys, what can I say? I was busy."

Vivi narrowed her eyes. "What kind of busy?"

Jack pretended he hadn't heard the question. "Huh?"

"I said, what kind of busy? What were you *doing* all week?"

Jack feigned innocence. "Nothing."

"You were doing literally *nothing*," said Vivi.

Jack shrugged. "Yeah. Pretty much. Just, you know. Taking stock."

Sampson sniggered. "Yeah. Taking stock of your balls."

"Dude," said Reese. "That doesn't even make sense."

Darylyn stared at Jack, wide-eyed.

Vivi wore a freaked out "ew" face. "Is that true?" she said.

Philo seemed to have tuned out of the whole conversation, but then he turned to Vivi and said, "Is what true?"

"Nothing," said Jack.

Philo nodded thoughtfully. "Interesting philosophical point you've raised there."

Sampson sniggered again. "Speaking of points being raised."

"Sampson, you're so immature," said Vivi.

"Let's just forget the whole thing," said Jack. "*Bigwigs* is over and done with, I tried to get Sampson out of a tricky situation by accepting who I am, I've made my apologies, everyone's friends again, and nobody's been shut away in their room masturbating for days on end."

There was an awkward silence, broken only by the sound of Reese saying "Dude . . ." under his breath.

Jack blinked. "I said 'masturbating,' didn't I?"

Everyone nodded.

Well I guess that's that, thought Jack.

Things hadn't really changed that much. This was how it was going to be.

Now that he'd hit the big time.

Acknowledgments

Thanks to my commissioning editor, Marisa Pintado, for her wit, wiles, and wisdom in nudging me toward writing a "straight" book instead of something with, you know, aliens in it. Thanks also to Hilary Rogers, Karri Hedge, Sarah Magee, Niki Horin, and everyone else at Hardie Grant Egmont for their commitment to and enthusiasm for this book. It is extraordinarily humbling.

Enormous thanks to Daniel Lazar at Writers House, and to David Gale, Gary Sunshine, Liz Kossnar, Lucy Ruth Cummins, Jenica Nasworthy, and everyone else at Simon & Schuster, for helping to bring *Spurt* to the United States.

Thanks to Myke Bartlett, Leanne Hall, and Andrew McDonald for workshopping get-togethers, invaluable advice, and writerly chats. You guys are like Bigwigs of the YA world to me. To desk-sharing writer-buddies Mat Larkin and Andrew McDonald (no relation to the previous Andrew

McDonald, except for the fact that they are the same person), thanks for keeping me honest and indulging my cravings for Lebanese pies.

Thanks to television's Kynan Barker and Josie Steele for invaluable early notes about "the biz" (including patiently explaining that nobody really calls it "the biz").

Thanks to Simon Haines, Cristina Pink-Charlton, and Sabdha Pink-Charlton for reading early versions of Jack's adventures and kindly refraining from saying terrible things about them.

Thanks to Jeremy Daly for dipping into his seemingly bottomless well of knowledge and producing the Calypso War phenomenon that Reese tells Jack about, and to Chris Gemmill for advising me on the logistics of modern Phys Ed. Thanks also to Peter Anderson for helping me choose the right wheels for Collinson Wade—a character who alas did not make the final draft. (Hopefully he will park his rented SsangYong Chairman in a future tale.)

Thanks to my mom and my late dad, my sister, and my daughter, for putting up with a son, a brother, and a father who spent—and spends—way too much time in his own head.

And lastly, everlasting thanks to Nikki for being my companion on this long road to publication—and more importantly, my companion on the journey toward the getting of wisdom, and everything else that lies ahead.